PHYLLIS REYNOLDS
NAYLOR

A CLUB OF MYSTERIES BOOK

Carlotta's Kittens

ILLUSTRATED BY ALAN DANIEL

ALADDIN PAPERBACKS
NEW YORK LONDON TORONTO SYDNEY SINGAPORE

First Aladdin Paperbacks edition February 2002

Aladdin Paperbacks
An imprint of Simon & Schuster
Children's Publishing Division
1230 Avenue of the Americas
New York, NY 10020

Also available in an Atheneum Books for Young Readers hardcover edition.
Designed by Jim Hoover
The text of this book was set in Goudy.
The illustrations were rendered in ink.

Printed in the United States of America
2 4 6 8 10 9 7 5 3 1

The Library of Congress has cataloged the hardcover edition as follows:
Naylor, Phyllis Reynolds.
Carlotta's kittens and the Club of Mysteries / Phyllis Reynolds Naylor
p. cm.
Summary: Continues the adventures of Marco, Polo, and other members of the Club of Mysteries as they care for Carlotta's kittens and search for a home for them.
ISBN 0-689-83269-9 (hc.)
[1. Cats—Fiction. 2. Adventure and adventurers—Fiction.] I. Title
PZ7.N24 Car 2000
[FIC]—dc21 99-57042
ISBN 0-689-83459-4 (Aladdin pbk.)

To Tressa and Sophia

and all their cousins

Contents

One: Asking Around 1
Two: *Oh, Carlotta!* 8
Three: Five Little Nothings 15
Four: The Secret is Out 20
Five: Naming the Nothings 27
Six: The Mystery of Heat 32
Seven: Lullaby 37
Eight: A Visit to the Kiwanis Club 46
Nine: A Lesson in the Fine Arts 50
Ten: Saving Your Skins 55
Eleven: Bad News 61
Twelve: Polite Inquiries 67
Thirteen: Walking the Line 75
Fourteen: Rescue Number One 80
Fifteen: On the Prowl 86
Sixteen: Into the Pipes 93
Seventeen: Steak Knife's Collection 100
Eighteen: A Little Disguise 109
Nineteen: The Kittens' Song 117
Twenty: Good-bye, Good-bye . . . 124

A Club of Mysteries Book

Carlotta's Kittens

One
Asking Around

When the air was cold, and the sky was gray, and the wind blew its frosty breath through every crack and crevice, Marco and Polo thought of Carlotta. The thick white snow beyond the window sparkled in the noonday sun. At night it glistened in the soft yellow light of the street-lamps. It silently snuggled up against doors and garden walls. And somewhere, they didn't know where, the beautiful calico cat was having her kittens.

"I wonder if she's safe," said Marco, the larger of the tabbies.

"I wonder if she's warm," said Polo, his brother, who was known, now and then, to chase his tail.

And they both wondered whether she was getting enough to eat, or whether she was eating anything at all. Being male cats, they had no idea what it was like to be called "Carlotta" one day, and "Mother" the next.

And then Marco said what they were both thinking:

"What if some other cat from the Club of Mysteries finds her first, and decides to be daddy to her kittens?"

All the cats in the Club of Mysteries wanted to be special in Carlotta's eyes. Each of them dreamed of someday doing something so brave, so noble, that the beautiful calico cat, who was a friend to all but the true love of none, would think him best. But none of them knew where she had gone to have her kittens, only that she was going. And now that autumn had changed to winter, and the world had turned to ice, the cats worried.

Marco crawled out of the velveteen basket and stretched himself, rump in the air. His belly was so round that it grazed the floor, and he opened his mouth and gave an enormous yawn.

"I think I'll trot over to the Club to see what's what," he said.

Polo tried to pretend he didn't hear. He tried to pretend he didn't see. When he dreamed of protecting Carlotta and her kittens, he rather imagined seeing them lined up outside the picture window, and that he would meow till his mistress let them in. He didn't think about actually going out after them. He didn't think *cold.* He didn't think *snow.* He didn't think *freeze your tail off and your whiskers too.*

Nonetheless, if Marco was going, Polo was going. He couldn't stand the thought of Marco finding the calico cat and snuggling up beside her, Polo not included. So he left the warmth of the velveteen basket too. When Jumper and Spinner, the kittens the Neals had adopted, saw them leaving, they asked, "When will *we* be old enough to join the Club of Mysteries?" for they had heard the tales of adventure the tabbies had told.

"Not for a long time yet," said Marco grandly. "A very long time." And with his tail in the air, he walked to the back door of the Neals' house, lifted his head, and yowled. Polo joined in.

"I hear you! I hear you!"Mrs. Neal said, coming in from the kitchen in her slippers. "I don't understand you two, I really don't. You wait until the coldest day of the year, and then you decide you want to go out prowling. Where you go and what you do is a mystery to me, because you have everything you could possibly want right inside these four walls."

Marco tried to tell her, but she never understood the language. He tried to explain it was the walls themselves they needed to escape from now and then, but the back door opened, and a moment later he and Polo stepped into three inches of snow. Polo started to back up, but with a nudge of her foot, Mrs. Neal propelled him off the step, and the door clicked behind him.

Marco lifted his right front paw and shook it, then his left front paw. He picked up his right hind foot and shook it, then his left. Polo tried to pick up three feet at one time and promptly fell on his nose.

"Why does it have to be so cold?" he asked, his teeth chattering. He always asked his brother these questions, because Marco could read. Somehow Marco had taught himself the alphabet while sitting in his litter box, studying the newspaper there at the bottom. Polo just did his business and climbed out.

"It is cold," said Marco, "because it is not hot. And the opposite of hot is cold."

“Oh,” Polo said, and wished for the twentieth time that he were even half as smart as his brother.

They delicately crossed the yard, stepping in the footprints made by Mr. Neal that morning when he had gone out to his car. Then they jumped up on the fence, over the gate, and down into the alley.

The mouse named Timothy scurried under a garbage-can lid when he saw them coming. He had an understanding with the tabby brothers that they would never harm him. Still, Marco forgot sometimes, and pounced. He’d hold the little mouse tight in his paws for a moment or two before letting him go, and Timothy would prefer not to go through that ordeal again.

The snow was dazzling in the morning sun, but not so dazzling that Polo didn’t see the mouse.

“Good morning, Timothy,” he called. “Have you seen Carlotta lately?”

“The calico she-cat with the plump belly?” asked Timothy. “I heard she went off somewhere to have her kittens.”

“But where?” asked Marco.

“Here . . . there . . . could be anywhere,” Timothy answered. “Mostly I just stay out of her way. Any she-cat who has just had kittens is hungry, and I don’t want to be on her menu.” And the little mouse disappeared.

The next creature the tabby brothers encountered was the black crow that scavenged around the neighborhood.

“Good morning,” called Marco. “Have you, by chance, seen Carlotta and her kittens?”

“Ah!” The crow stopped picking at a dead squirrel on the pavement and fixed his eye on Marco. Marco and Polo were trying not to look at the squirrel. "She's had her kittens, has she? Well, if she doesn't take care, one will get run over by a car, one will die of cold, one will die of hunger, one will get attacked by a vicious dog, and I shall have my choice of dishes for a week."

"How can you say such things?" cried Polo. "Doesn't it ruin your appetite?"

"Not at all, not at all," said the crow. "We are the street cleaners—pickers, if you will—of society. One day a possum is dead upon the highway, and the next it's gone. And who has come by to clean up the mess? Your friendly, efficient neighborhood crow, that's who."

"But you *haven't* seen them, have you? You haven't breakfasted on fillet of kitten, I hope?" Marco asked.

"No, but if you see Carlotta, tell her to keep her kittens close to her at all times, especially when crossing the street. A flat cat is of no use whatsoever to its mother, but it *does* make a tasty pancake."

At this the tabbies were more determined than ever to find their calico friend, and finally they reached Murphy's garage, where the Club of Mysteries held its meetings. It wasn't too long ago that Marco and Polo had become members, having successfully solved one of life's great mysteries that Texas Jake, the leader, had assigned them—namely, where does water go when it rains? They had never felt that the big yellow cat approved of them 100 percent. But Murphy's garage was as good a place as any to get out of the wind, catch up on neighborhood gossip, and—most important—see Carlotta. And so they crept inside and up the dusty stairs to the loft above. There they discovered a meeting already in progress; no one had waited for them.

On an old rocking chair in the center of the floor sat the big yellow cat, the scars from many battles on his skin. Texas Jake inched himself forward until both his nose and his claws were overhanging the seat of the chair, and glowered at Marco and Polo with his huge yellow eyes.

"Well, well, lads, look what we have here! Our two newest members. We thought for sure we had frightened you off," he said.

"Never," said Marco, prepared to take his place with the best of them. "We wondered if anyone has seen Carlotta, and whether or not she has had her kittens."

"We're all wondering the same thing," said Boots, the smallest of the cats, with brown on the ends of his four white paws. "The last any of us has seen of her was the day she announced she was going away for a while and did not want to be disturbed."

"I have even been by her master's home, and heard him calling her, but she didn't come," said Elvis, a coal-black cat with green eyes.

"Then here's what we shall do," said Texas Jake, Commander in Chief, King of the Alley, Lord of the Loft, the Cat Supreme. "Everyone knows that new kittens are in danger until they're old enough to take care of themselves, and it's up to us to protect Carlotta and her litter. Boots, you look for her tracks in the snow; Elvis, you watch for her at the Fishmonger; and *you,*" he said, turning to the tabbies, "must stand guard outside the door to Murphy's garage—sentinels, if you will. Keep your eyes on the alley and your ears to the wind, and report back to me twice a day."

"And you, Texas Jake. What will *you* do?" asked Marco boldly.

The big cat rolled his eyes one way, then rolled them the other. "I'll wait until you bring Carlotta and her kittens to me," he said. "*Then*, my lads, we will decide what is what."

Two
Oh, Carlotta!

"Why is it," Polo wondered aloud, "that no matter what the plan, Texas Jake always seems to get the best of things? While we're out in the cold looking for Carlotta, he's snoozing up in the loft."

"The reason," said Marco, "is that *he* makes the plans. As Lord of the Loft, Commander in Chief, King of the Alley, and Cat Supreme, he makes sure that the best of everything goes to him with as little work on his part as possible."

"But we don't even get to move around," Polo complained. "We're just supposed to stand out here like soldiers freezing our tails off."

"We'll see about that," said Marco. "What *I* think is that if we're going to be the ones who find Carlotta, we have to think like a she-cat. If *you* were about to have kittens, Polo, where would *you* go?"

"Back to my velveteen basket," Polo answered.

"Well, since her master's out looking for her, she's obviously not home. Try again," said Marco.

"I suppose I'd make myself a nest high in a tree where dogs couldn't get my kittens," Polo decided.

"Fine! And the first big storm that came along would shake the tree and it would rain kittens!" Marco told him. "*Think*, Polo. *Think!*"

"I would want to find a place that was dry and warm and safe and . . . and private. Very private," Polo decided.

"Right," said Marco. "And *that's* why it's going to be so hard to find her. In the meantime, let's head for the Fishmonger. Texas Jake didn't say we couldn't eat, and I now declare it suppertime."

Everyone else had the same idea, because all the other cats were there except Carlotta, even cats who weren't members of the Club.

It was Friday; Fish Day at the restaurant—"all you can eat"—and the great thing about "all you can eat" was that the two-leggeds who came to the restaurant always thought they could eat more than they did. They would heap their plates with salmon steak and fillet of sole, with a few fried scallops on the side, and a lot would get left over and thrown away. And that, of course, was a banquet for the cats.

"Marco! Polo! Where have you been?" called the Siamese in his mournful voice. "We haven't seen you for a while."

"It's been cold," said Polo. "And our velveteen basket is warm."

"True, but it's warm down in the garbage can along with all the fish," said the Persian with the huge fluffy tail. "My master hates it when I come home smelling like flounder, but I tell you, it's a smell that warms the soul."

"What we need," said Marco, "is a smell that warms the feet."

"Never mind the feet. What we need is a bottom

warmer. How they expect us to sit out here feasting on left-overs in three inches of snow is a mystery to me," the Abyssinian said.

"Less talk and more eating!" thundered Texas Jake, tired of all the complaining. "Heads down and tails up, lads! And when you're through, perhaps we could have a little music with our meal."

"Hear! Hear!" the cats all cried, and Elvis's eyes shone, for he liked nothing better than to sing in front of an admiring audience there in the parking lot.

Soon the air was filled with the sounds of snacking, smacking, snarling, slurping, sipping, snapping, sucking, swilling. Every fishy flake was swallowed, every bitty bone licked dry, and finally, when the cats began cleaning their paws and rubbing their ears and whiskers, Elvis crawled up on the wall at the back of the parking lot and began warming up.

"A song! A song!" the other cats cried, huddling together for warmth, but hating to leave before the evening's entertainment.

"To my fellow felines," Elvis said. "Because we have all been missing a certain somebody, I have composed a song called 'Oh, Carlotta!'" And to the tune of "Oh, Susannah!", Elvis sang:

"Oh, I come from Al-abama
With the mange upon my knee,
I'm a-goin' to Lou-siana
My Carlotta for to see.

"It snowed so hard, I froze my toes,
The ice was hard and slick,

The wind so strong, it cleaned my nose,
And almost made me sick.

"Oh, Car-lotta!
We miss your purr so dear,
If we knew where to find you now,
We'd go and bring you here."

The other cats meowed their delight, and then the Abyssinian, the Siamese, and the Persian climbed up on the fence beside Elvis for the finale. The cat quartet practiced a few notes in private, and at last agreed upon a second verse, which they sang most lustily:

"I had a dream the other night,
The snow so white and soft,
I thought I saw Carlotta dear
A-comin' to the loft.

"The salmon cake was in her mouth,
The dust was in her eye,
She said she was a mother now,
We're all as pleased as pie."

And this time, when they got to the chorus, all the cats in the parking lot joined in:

"Oh, Car-lotta!
We miss your purr so dear,
If we knew where to find you now,
We'd go and bring you here."

"Ah, well," said Texas Jake, getting stiffly to his feet to signal an end to the festivities. "If singing could bring her back, she'd be here now. Motherhood, lads, is a deep dark secret the likes of us will never know."

The crowd of cats began to leave. Texas Jake, Elvis, Boots, Marco, and Polo all went back to Murphy's loft. None of the cats, Marco noticed, was going home to his master or mistress, because all wanted to be on hand when Carlotta did come. But who knew when that would be?

"Soooo," said Texas Jake, looking around, "we are all staying here for the night? None of us is going home to his warm bed and little tin of gourmet food?"

In answer, Boots and Elvis climbed up on the old army cot where they often slept. Marco and Polo were about to join them when Texas Jake gave them a swat with his large paw. "You are on guard duty, are you not?" he hissed. "You may take turns sleeping, if you must, but one of you must be on the lookout for Carlotta at all times."

Marco gave a low hiss but slunk back. "We will stand guard, Texas Jake, but it will be in here at the top of the stairs. A frozen cat is no good to you at all."

"Very well," said Texas, "but make sure the guard doesn't get a little too comfortable, a little too drowsy."

"I'll take the first shift," Marco said to Polo, leaping up on a pile of magazines beside the top step.

Polo didn't protest, but gratefully jumped up on the army cot beside Boots and Elvis and closed one eye. But Marco sat upright, ears and eyes alert.

Texas Jake studied him from his perch on the rocker.

"Any idea how long it takes for kittens to be born, Marco—since you are the cat who can reeeaaad?" he asked, drawing out the word. "A cat who can reeeaaad should know something about birth and could educate us."

"I'm afraid not," said Marco. "I don't do much medical reading."

"A pity," said Texas. "A pity." And he stretched his long body out on the seat of the rocker, laid his head to one side, and with a great sigh, closed his eyes.

It was cold and drafty in the loft, and Marco shivered at his station by the stairs. He watched the other cats snuggled warmly against each other, their paws twitching now and then. But he himself could only listen to the wind blowing through the small window at one end.

When the first rays of light entered the loft, Marco was dismayed to discover that he had dozed off in spite of himself, and he hastily straightened his back and snapped his jaws together, looking as alert as possible. Something had awakened him, he wasn't sure what. Over on the army cot, Polo, too, opened his eyes. What was it? A paw-step, perhaps. The creak of a stair. Texas Jake suddenly sat up, and Boots and Elvis sprang to attention. All lifted their heads expectantly.

And then the paw-steps came again, and as the cats watched in wonder, Carlotta appeared at the top of the stairs, holding a wee kitten in her mouth by the scruff of its neck. Before the cats could speak, she gently dropped it into a box of rags and disappeared back down the stairs.

Again she came, and again and again, each time with another teeny kitten in her mouth, until there were five tiny squirming, mewing, wriggling little balls of fur on top of an old flannel shirt in the rag box.

"Hello," said Carlotta. "I'm back!"

Three

Five Little Nothings

Polo had imagined that when Carlotta came back, every cat in the Club of Mysteries would greet her with cries of delight.

But the loft had never been more quiet. There was only the faintest sound of five little kittens mewing there in the rag box, and then, as she laid herself down beside them, the tired but happy purr of Carlotta.

Slowly, slowly, the he-cats moved down from their perches on the rocking chair, the army cot, and the pile of old magazines.

Reverently they gathered around Carlotta and her litter, but not too close, as the kittens buried their noses in her warm fur and drank her milk.

Happily, gratefully, they listened to the purr they knew and loved, and then Texas Jake spoke for all of them: "Welcome back, Carlotta, and all your kittens too."

"We missed you," said Marco.

"Your purr . . . ," said Polo.

"Your fur . . . ," said Boots.

"The little flip of your tail," said Elvis.

"I've missed you too. But now I am very, very tired, and wish to sleep," said Carlotta.

The he-cats gathered over by the stairs so as not to disturb her.

"Do you see how tired she is?" said Texas Jake to the others. "Do you see how helpless and small her kittens are? One of us must always be here to protect them, and I will take that upon myself. What will the rest of you do to help?"

"We will bring her food," said Marco.

"And help bring up her kittens," said Boots.

"And teach them songs," said Elvis.

"That's well and good," said Texas Jake, "but nobody else, *no*body, must know they're here. And that, my lads, will be the hardest job of all."

"Why?" asked Polo.

"Why?" Texas repeated. "*Why*? Where were you when the brains were passed around, Polo? Have you never heard of the pound?"

Of course Polo knew about the pound. You could hardly be called a cat if you did not know what went on there.

"You mean someone would take her babies away?" he asked. He knew that unwanted animals were sometimes "put to sleep," as the two-leggeds called it, but he did not know they did that to kittens too.

"Every last one of them," said Texas. "They wouldn't drown them, of course. They'd wait a week or two to see if anyone came in wanting a kitten. But then, if no one adopted them, they'd slip them a needle, and *zap*. Gone."

"But why? *Why?*" Polo wanted to know.

"They say there are getting to be too many of us," said Marco, having read all about it in the newspapers. "They say that every responsible pet owner should have his cat or dog fixed so they can't produce any more babies. So we won't even *want* to."

All the cats began to hiss at once, but with a single glance toward Carlotta, Texas Jake quieted them immediately.

"I know a few families *I'd* like to fix," said Boots. "Why, there's a family of ten kids who live on my block, and every time they see me, every last one of them tries to pull my tail."

"It's not cats who are polluting the rivers," said Elvis.

"It's not cats who pollute the air. Did you ever see a cat smoking?" asked Texas.

"It's not cats who are cutting down the rain forest, either," said Marco, but then he realized that none of the others knew what he was talking about, because he was the only cat who could read.

The he-cats listened to the soft little sounds of kittens drinking, and wondered about the fairness of a universe in which humans got to decide who would live and who would die.

"Think of it!" said Texas after a bit. "A man comes into the pound with a dog who tears up his slippers, or a cat who scratches his couch. 'I can't keep him anymore,' the man says, 'because he's ruining my house.' And the lady at the pound gets to decide what to do with the animal. Put him to sleep right away, give him a ten-day reprieve, or what."

"What *I'd* like to do," said Elvis, "is sit behind the desk in a people pound. When a Siamese brought in a master and complained that he never fixed his supper on time, I'd say, 'Over there, in that cage. We'll give him seven days to straighten out. If not, he'll get the needle.'"

"Oh, I'd love to do that too!" said Marco. "All day long I'd make pronouncements. 'Your master snores? Give him the needle.' 'Your mistress puts you out in the rain? Ten days of solitary confinement.' Too big, too small, too short, too tall. I'd find fault with everyone, and the two-leggeds would tremble in my presence."

Again the cats fell into thoughtful silence, mulling over the mystery of the pound.

"It comes down to this, lads," Texas Jake said at last. "If we could use a can opener and open a door, we'd have it made. Those are the only two things humans really have to do for us. If we could open our own food and our own doors, we could eat where we pleased, go out and in as suited us best, and never ask a single thing of humans."

"We could, of course, catch our own food, sleep in the woods, and never go near a door or a can opener. Then we wouldn't need humans at all," Marco said. But none of the others thought much of that idea.

"No, lads, this is probably as good as it will get for us, and we'd better be grateful we each have a home," Texas said.

As if the Universe were listening, a ray of sun came through the window at the far end of the loft and made a patch of yellow on the floor. One by one each cat went over and lay down in it, vying for room, all except Polo, who was now on watch by the stairs. They sunned themselves and licked their paws and wondered what kind of world it would be for Carlotta's kittens when they were older. *If* they were lucky enough to grow older, that is.

"Five little nothings, that's all they are to the folks at the pound," said Texas Jake. "Five little balls of fur of no real use whatsoever except to make us love them."

But the five big cats in the Club of Mysteries knew that if Carlotta was special, so were her kittens. The problem wasn't just to keep them that way. The problem was, first, to keep them secret, and second, to keep them alive.

Four

The Secret is Out

While Polo served as lookout on the stairs that day, and Texas Jake stood guard over Carlotta and her five kittens, Marco, Boots, and Elvis went to the Fishmonger and each brought back a tasty morsel, laying it carefully on the floor outside the rag box. Carlotta was awake now, and left her little brood long enough to eat a piece of fried perch and a few shrimp. Then she went downstairs to get some water from outside.

The five little nothings mewed pitifully when she left. Their eyes were still closed and they wriggled about on the old flannel shirt, squeaking out their frustration.

"Look at them!" whispered Elvis. "They're blind! Do you think Carlotta knows? They're bumping into each other!"

"And there's something wrong with their voices. They squeak!" said Polo.

"Their legs are like flippers," observed Marco. "They

can't even stand up; they just flop around on their bellies."

"She's got a bad batch here, lads, but who's going to tell her?" said Texas Jake, peering over the side of the box. "Poor Carlotta."

"Why? What's the matter?"

The he-cats jumped when they realized that Carlotta had come back up the stairs and was standing just behind them. They parted to let her pass, and she climbed back into the box again where she lay on her side, licking her paws and cleaning her whiskers, while the five kittens squirmed and squealed and burrowed their noses into the fur on her belly.

"So, what's wrong with my kittens?" she asked.

The he-cats looked at each other, none wishing to be the bearer of bad news.

"Well," said Elvis finally. "It appears as though . . . well, something may be wrong with their eyes."

"And their mew-boxes," said Polo.

"And their legs," said Marco.

"It's a terrible shock, I know, my dear, but I'm afraid you've got yourself a bad litter," Texas told her.

Carlotta lifted her head, her green eyes like ice, and stared at the five male cats hulking over her.

"You may be big," she said, "and you may be strong, but you've all got the brains of a banana. Little kittens are *supposed* to be this way when they're born. Their eyes don't open for at least ten days. Their voices and their legs get stronger every day. But for now, it's all up to me. If anything happened to me, I don't know what would become of my kittens."

"We'll protect you, Carlotta," Marco told her. "You can count on us."

"*All* of us," said Texas Jake, refusing to let Marco take the credit.

"Thank you," said Carlotta. "The breakfast was delicious, and I appreciate you all, but now I think I would like a nap." And she laid her head down and was soon sound asleep beside her kittens.

The other cats gathered around Texas Jake's rocker to let Carlotta and her kittens sleep, while Polo stood sentinel by the stairs. Of all the cats, it was Polo who most missed his mother. Were he ever to see her again, of course, he didn't even know what she would look like. All he could remember was something large and warm and soft, with a deep rumbling purr and a dank milky scent. But what he would give to smell it again!

The other cats seemed to be thinking of their mothers too, because Polo heard Elvis say, "The earliest memory I have is sitting out in the barn with my brothers and sisters, howling and yowling till we were quite hoarse. Our mother always told us we could probably have lived right there on the farm for the rest of our lives if we hadn't made so much noise, but would we listen? No."

"The only way I escaped the pound was by running away," said Boots. "There were six in our litter. I don't remember being blind or squeaking, but I do remember the day my mistress boxed us up to go to the pound. At the last minute I jumped over the side as she put us in her car. I ran and ran and she never did find me. My current master found me sitting on his doorstep and liked my paws. 'Boots,' he called them, and took me in.

If it weren't for my brown paws, I might have starved."

For all his learning, Marco could not remember his early days as a young kitten. But he remembered being in the pound—how he had hoped someone would adopt him—and how lucky he had felt when the Neals took both him and Polo.

It was Texas Jake's story that bothered them most, however.

"It's like this, lads," he said. "I was born in an alley of a mother who didn't want us, not a one. She stayed around just long enough to get us weaned, and then she was off to who knows where, and the six of us wandered around trash cans, eating whatever we could find. Two of us got run over, one of us was killed by a dog, and finally a man comes out with a gunnysack, tosses the last three of us in it, takes us down to the river, and throws us in."

The other cats gasped in horror.

"Well, he was pretty good at tossing the bag, but he wasn't so good at tying it, and when it hit the water, the end came open, and somehow I got to shore."

No one wanted to ask the next question, but finally Elvis asked it: "What happened to the other two?"

"I don't know. Lost, I suppose," Texas told him.

The loft was very, very quiet.

"Do you suppose they're right? The pound people?" asked Boots at last. "Maybe there *are* too many of us. And if we can't take care of ourselves, and the two-leggeds can't take care of us all, then maybe it's time that we—well, *some* of us, anyway—should be fixed so we can't make so many kittens."

A shudder went through the little group.

"Not white cats with brown paws, of course," Boots said.

"Or black cats with green eyes," said Elvis.

"Or yellow cats with white bellies," said Texas.

"Or tabbies . . . " said Marco.

"Especially brothers," put in Polo, over by the stairs.

"Or Carlotta," all the he-cats said at once.

Suddenly, far down below, came a sound that caused Polo to prick up his ears. He left the group of he-cats in the loft and edged his body a step at a time down the staircase until he could see the floor of Murphy's garage. He listened.

The noise was distant at first, growing louder and louder—the rattle of a chain leash, perhaps. And finally the unmistakable thud of dog steps and the running of human feet.

The hair on Polo's back began to rise, his spine began to arch, his tail to thicken.

"Bertram!" came a man's voice. "What's got into you, buddy? What do you smell?"

Bertram the Bad, the huge mastiff who lived down the block, was going for a walk with his master. Or rather, the master was going for a walk with his dog. For when Polo peeped out the garage door, the great animal was coming full speed toward Murphy's garage, half dragging the man behind him.

Like lightning, Polo raced up the stairs and had just time enough to hiss, "Bertram," when the monster of a dog flung himself into Murphy's garage and, breaking loose from his master, his nose quivering with the scent of kittens, started up the stairs.

He was met with a wall of cats, a web of claws, a fence

of jagged cat teeth, all attacking at the same time. A claw to the right ear, a bite to the left. Polo went for the nose, and Texas Jake took his flank. The air was filled with yips and yowls, with hisses and howls, until finally the master had the dog by the collar once more and was dragging him out of the garage.

"Bad dog! Bad dog! Bad, bad, bad!" said the master, swatting Bertram on the head.

The cats slowly picked themselves up, licking their wounds and checking their body parts to be sure none were missing. On the very top step, they found Carlotta, lying as still as a sweater on the arm of a chair.

"Carlotta?" Marco gasped. "Carlotta was fighting too?"

"To the death," said Texas Jake, panting still. "A she-cat will fight to the death to save her kittens."

The he-cats quickly gathered around, licking the head of the calico cat until at last she stirred and opened her eyes.

"I'm all right," she said, "but thank you for helping to save my kittens."

"You should have let us protect you," Boots told her. "Leave the fighting to us."

Carlotta slowly got to her feet. "You don't understand," she said. "When my kittens are in danger, I *have* to fight. It's as much a part of me as breathing."

The he-cats accompanied her back to the rag box where her hungry kittens waited. No one spoke, but the members of the Club of Mysteries exchanged glances, and each knew what the others were thinking: If Bertram knew, then it was only a matter of time before everyone in the alley and beyond would know that Carlotta's tender, pink-nosed, milk-stained, silk-eared kittens had come.

Five
Naming the Nothings

None of the he-cats dared go home, for if Carlotta and her kittens were in trouble, every cat would be needed. Carlotta herself stayed very still and quiet, and seemed to need a lot of sleep. She ate the food the other cats brought her from the Fishmonger, and she was content to lie in the rag box and nurse her kittens. Her deep purr was music up in the loft.

Every day, however, the kittens' own squeaks and squeals grew a little louder. Every day their legs seemed stronger. Their eyes were still closed, but they pushed more vigorously when trying to get to their mother to nurse, and they sounded more indignant when she left them to go outside now and then. Marco and Polo loved to sit nearby and just watch, for when the kittens were asleep, they sprawled every which way on Carlotta's belly, and when they were awake, they were a three-ring circus, tumbling and sliding and sneezing and bumping.

One kitten was calico, just like Carlotta—red and brown and black and white, like a patchwork quilt.

One kitten was mostly black with white patches.

One was mostly white with black patches.

One was brown with white paws.

And the last, the smallest of all, was a yellow cat with white stripes.

When the day came that the kittens' eyes were open, their eleventh day, none of the he-cats wanted to leave long enough to go to the Fishmonger, for the kittens stared at each other in wonder. They looked at Carlotta as though she were a magnificent mountain to climb, and were endlessly fascinated with their own bodies, jumping at the sight of their own tails trailing along behind them.

As for the five members of the Club of Mysteries, the kittens tried to hide whenever a he-cat came into view. They burrowed under Carlotta or down in the corners of the rag box, and more than once they got stuck headfirst and had to be pulled out by their mother.

"You know," said Texas Jake, "they are soon going to be strong enough to crawl out of that box."

"And curious enough to climb down the stairs," said Boots.

"And loud enough to be heard from below," said Marco.

"And big enough to fall out a window," said Elvis.

"And hungry enough to need more than milk," said Polo.

"It is time," said Texas, "to give the nothings some names. What about it, Carlotta? Have you decided yet on names for your kittens?"

But Carlotta said, "I don't know my kittens by names, I know them by smell. One smells more like milk than fur, one smells more like fur than feet, one smells more like feet than ears, one smells more like ears than eyes, and one smells like tail. Definitely tail. That's how I know my kittens."

"Still," said Marco, "if we needed to call them in a hurry, we should know their names."

"Then you fellows name them yourselves, whatever you'd like," Carlotta told them.

The members of the Club of Mysteries gathered around the box and each chose one of the kittens to name. Texas Jake chose the largest kitten and named it Hamburger.

Elvis chose the wiggliest of the kittens and named it Scamper.

Marco chose the yellowest of the kittens and named it Mustard.

Boots chose the kitten with the most white in its fur and named it Sugar.

Polo chose the smallest and named it Catnip.

"They sound more like a grocery list than kittens," Carlotta said.

But Hamburger, Scamper, Mustard, Sugar, and Catnip all snuggled up against their mother, oblivious to the fact that they could not stay there forever, that there was a big, wide world to explore.

Marco awoke the next morning to find the air warmer. Definitely warmer. He yawned and stretched himself, and trotted over to Polo, who was standing guard at the stairs.

"Is it spring?" he asked. "Have I been hibernating?"

Polo gave him a sleepy look. "No, it is the morning of an unusually warm day, and I would like nothing better than to take a nap."

Marco stuck his nose down the stairs and sniffed. Polo was right. It wasn't spring, just a January thaw—those wonderful few days that lull the two-leggeds into thinking that winter is over, so they put their snow shovels away and are bamboozled once again by a snowstorm.

"Tell you what," Marco said to his brother. "Let me go for a short walk in this magnificent sunshine, and then I'll be back to relieve you."

So he went down the stairs of Murphy's garage, out into the alley, down the block, across the street, and started along the alley on the other side. The sunshine was glorious, the air was warm, and birds, which had not made a peep since October, were trilling out their songs from the rooftops.

Marco had fully intended to stop off at the Fishmonger first for a bite of breakfast, but the exercise felt so good after lying around the loft that his paws kept going until the ground of the alley gave way to dirt. He began to slow down. He had never come this far by himself before; Polo had always been at his side. He realized that he was heading toward the city dump where Steak Knife and his gang hung out, and knew that he should not go another step farther. If he suddenly turned on his heels, however, wouldn't it look as though he were running away? For surely he was being watched that very minute. He had never before thought he needed his brother for courage, but he wished Polo were with him now. What would Polo say, he wondered, if Marco said they could hardly turn around now and run?

We could always walk backward. That was probably what Polo would say, and it just might make sense. And then he heard voices up ahead.

One came from a hollow stump: "So I've heard . . . Carlotta's had her kittens . . . ."

And from a tree: "But no one knows where they are."

From a clump of leaves on the ground: "Oh, how I'd like to sink my teeth into a tender kitten. . . . "

And from a hollow log, the most raggedy voice of all: " . . . and a tail for my collection, to hang on the fence at the dump. I've got rat tails, cat tails, dog tails, squirrel tails, but not the tail of a kitten."

Marco began to walk backward, and then he turned and ran. Faster and faster, away from the trees, down the dirt path, his feet like wheels, tail in the air, and he did not stop until he had reached the street.

Six
The Mystery of Heat

The message was borne on the wind, it seemed. It traveled from tree to fence to trash can to alley. *Carlotta's kittens had come, and were somewhere in the neighborhood, no one knew quite where.* Except for the members of the Club of Mysteries, that is.

Marco raced up the stairs to the loft of Murphy's garage to tell the news, and found the other cats awake and discussing what each would teach the kittens to do.

"I'll teach them to hunt," said Texas Jake grandly. "A cat who can hunt will never be thin."

"I'll teach them to sing," said Elvis. "A cat who can sing will never be sad."

"Never mind hunting and singing," Marco exclaimed, still panting. "I have just come back from a stroll near the dump, and Steak Knife knows that the kittens have come. I heard the Over the Hill gang talking."

He hadn't wanted Carlotta to know—did not want to upset her—but she heard anyway.

"That's always the way it is with kittens," she said. "Everyone wants to get rid of them. That's the only reason my master adopted me; someone was giving me away, and maybe he felt sorry for me. But he doesn't want any more cats, that's certain. If he finds them, no telling what he will do."

"How can we help?" asked Elvis.

"Help me find good homes for them when they're old enough to leave. Help me protect them until then, and make them wise and strong so they can take care of themselves when they have to," Carlotta said.

"I will teach them safety," said Boots. "How to look both ways before crossing the street."

"I'll teach them to leap," called Polo from his post by the stairs. "A cat who can leap is sometimes the only cat left."

Texas Jake, from his perch on the rocker, cast a scornful glance in Marco's direction. "And what will *you* teach them, O Cat-Who-Can-Reeeaaad?" he asked.

"It wouldn't hurt them to know a few words," said Marco. "Words like 'Beware of the Dog,' maybe, and 'Keep Out.'"

"You are all kind to care so much for my kittens," said Carlotta, her eyes closing as she snuggled down with her litter again. She began to purr, and each of her kittens purred—little rattling noises like marbles bouncing around in the bottom of a tea kettle.

Marco and Polo exchanged places, and while Marco stood guard over the stairs, the older cats talked about how to find good homes for Carlotta's kittens.

"If *I* could choose the perfect home," said Texas Jake, "it would have a separate door so that I could go in and out at will."

"I have that already," said Carlotta. "But it's not the perfect home. Master says I'm not to bring any other cats with me, and that includes kittens. What is a home if you can't have your friends and relatives in to visit?"

"If *I* could design the perfect home for a cat, it would have a special door into the refrigerator!" said Boots.

"Yes! Yes!" meowed all the cats together.

"If *I* were to design the perfect house, there would be tree branches growing across the ceiling in every room," said Carlotta. "Then I could walk from branch to branch, room to room, to look down on my master and see what he was doing."

"I'd prefer a cave," said Polo. "*I* would have a magnificent cave built into the wall of the Neals' living room, a large dark hole where I could hide and look out at the world."

"There is a large dark hole in the wall of the Neals' living room, and you got into trouble once for going in there," Marco reminded him.

Polo tried to remember. "Oh, yes, the fireplace," he said.

"And you tracked ashes all over their white carpet," Marco added.

Elvis stretched himself and extended his claws in a delicious daydream. Then he opened one eye and said, "If *I* were to design a house, I would build a stage in one corner of the living room. I would have a spotlight shining just on me, and I would practice all my songs in the warmth of my home. I would not have to sit out on a cold fence waiting for an audience to arrive."

"That's what all cats should have—a little lever to push

that makes a house warmer or cooler," said Boots. "Why, if I had a lever to push, my master's house would be so warm that he would have to go around all January in his underpants."

"There is a knob on the wall of my master's house, and all he has to do is turn it to make the house warm," said Carlotta. "What makes heat? Does anyone know?"

"Lightning, of course," said Elvis.

"That's the stupidest thing I ever heard," said Texas Jake.

"Then where *does* heat come from?" asked Elvis.

"From energy," Marco answered, unable to be quiet any longer. He knew a lot of things the other cats didn't because he could read. "The two-leggeds build power plants to make electricity, and electricity is what makes heat come on in your houses."

"Wrong! Wrong! Wrong!" hissed Texas, rising up on the rocking chair and glaring at Marco. "That is even more stupid than the lightning-bolt story. I'm surprised that Marco, the cat who can reeeeaaaaad"—and here Texas Jake drew the word out to a ridiculous length—"doesn't know any more than that."

Marco was confused. It was true that the story of electricity was complicated, and perhaps he didn't have it exactly right, but still, he *had* read about power plants, and he *had* read about electricity. "Then what does make heat?" he asked Texas Jake.

The big yellow cat looked disdainfully down at the others assembled there on the floor.

"Where does the heat come out in your masters' houses?" he asked. "Near the ceiling or the floor?"

"The floor," meowed all the cats together.

"And if you were to go in the basement of your masters' homes, to what are the heat pipes connected?"

"To the furnace," said Polo, glad that he knew the answer for once.

"Brilliant lad," said Texas sarcastically. "And the furnace is next to the ground, is it not? Do you know *why* that is so, lads? Because under the furnace, and through the ground, is a pipe that leads to the very center of the earth where it is hottest of all."

Marco was surprised that Texas knew so much.

"Is it even hotter inside the earth than on the sun?" asked Polo.

"Of *course* it is hotter than the sun," Texas Jake answered. "If we heated our houses from the sun, all our furnaces would be on the roof, with pipes reaching up to the sky. Look about you, lads. Be observant. Use your heads. Just because a cat can reeeeaaad doesn't mean he knows everything."

"I guess not," said Marco enviously, because Carlotta was looking at Texas adoringly. If only *he* could do something brave and noble for Carlotta's kittens! If only *he* could be a hero in her eyes. As he studied the male cats around him, however, he realized that they all felt that way. They all wanted Carlotta to like them best.

Perhaps soon, very soon, Marco was thinking, he would be called upon to help save her kittens, and if he was, he hoped he would be ready.

Seven
Lullaby

As the kittens grew older, they slept less and played more. They were crawling out of the rag box now, then mewing to get back in. When one woke, they all woke, and it was hard to get them to sleep again.

It was also difficult to think about teaching the squirming little kittens anything. There was so much for them to learn, and so little time to do it before they would be out on their own.

One afternoon, as the he-cats set out for lunch, leaving Polo as lookout, Marco stopped so suddenly that Boots bumped into him from behind, then Elvis and Texas Jake.

"What is it?" the others asked, and then they saw what he was looking at. It was Carlotta's picture on a poster. The poster was on a telephone pole, and under the picture it said:

Missing Cat

Calico cat
About four years old
Possibly pregnant

Beneath that was the name and telephone number of her master.

"Great!" said Texas Jake. "Now everyone in the neighborhood will be looking for her."

"Even if our best friends ask—the Persian, the Abyssinian, and the Siamese—we must not tell them she's back," said Elvis. "Let's just say we're looking for her too."

"She's so lovely in that picture," said Marco longingly.

It must have been taken at Christmas, for it was a picture of Carlotta in front of a Christmas tree with a pink bow attached to her head and a sparkly collar around her neck.

At the Fishmonger, other cats had seen the poster also, and though none of them could read, they guessed what it meant.

"Do you suppose she's been cat-napped?" asked the Abyssinian.

"And being held for ransom?" asked the Siamese. "Her collar alone would be worth something."

But some cats suspected worse.

"Maybe she died giving birth to her kittens and they all died along with her," said one.

"Someday she will show up, I'm sure of it," said Texas Jake. "Let us concentrate on eating, lads, so we will all be in good health and spirits when the calico cat returns." And the members of the Club of Mysteries left the trash cans that afternoon each with a little something in his mouth for Carlotta, so there was no meowing till they got back to the loft.

"Such wonderful friends I have!" Carlotta purred as she nibbled on the delicacies in front of her—a piece of fried perch, a little broiled scrod, a couple of scallops, a French-fried potato, and a lobster claw.

It had indeed been a delicious meal at the Fishmonger, and afterward the he-cats sprawled out on the last patch of sunshine coming through the loft window, one cat's head on another's belly, that cat's paw on another's neck, that cat's neck on another's tail, and so it went—five happy cats, counting Carlotta, happily drifting off into satisfied slumber—while Polo stood guard at the stairs.

The kittens, however, had been sleeping most of the day and weren't feeling tired at all. In fact, having just nursed and refreshed themselves before the he-cats got back, they were feeling much invigorated, and began skittering across the floor like Ping-Pong balls.

Marco felt something run over his leg.

Polo felt something land on his tail.

Elvis got pummeled on the nose, Boots on the ear, but it wasn't until Hamburger landed on Texas Jake's belly that the big yellow cat sat up and bellowed, "Quiet!"

The fact was, Texas Jake may have been Lord of the Loft, Commander in Chief, King of the Alley, and Cat Supreme to the others, but he was just another big fur-bag to the kittens, who were afraid of nothing now as long as their mother was nearby.

"Carlotta," said Texas Jake, giving her a nudge, "make your kittens go to sleep."

"But they're not sleepy, Texas," she purred. "How can they sleep if they're not sleepy?"

"Well, *make* them sleepy!" the big cat said irritably. "Sing them a lullaby."

"I'm afraid I don't know any," the calico cat replied. "A mother's purr is the only lullaby a newborn needs, but when they're older, I'm afraid that something more is necessary."

"Elvis," said Texas, "I want you to compose a lullaby for Carlotta's kittens, and do it fast."

Elvis loved to be commissioned to write a song. So while the other cats slept with one eye open to look out for scampering kittens, and Polo stood guard at the stairs, Elvis climbed up on the old army cot to compose his lullaby.

At last he said it was ready. Texas Jake ordered all the kittens back to the rag box, and when five little faces were peering over the edge and ten velvety ears were listening, Elvis sang:

> "Rock-a-bye, kittens,
> In your soft beds,
> Texas commands you,
> 'Lay down your heads!'
> You must obey
> And sleep one and all,
> Or out goes the rag box
> Kittens and all."

Five little faces disappeared from sight; ten little ears followed. For a while the loft was as quiet as the alley on Sunday mornings. But after a while, Scamper got a little adventurous, followed by Mustard and Catnip, and they were at it once again.

So Elvis added a second verse:

"Rock-a-bye, kittens,
Looping the loop,
If you don't stop,
We'll make kitten soup.
If you're not still,
We'll start you to roast,
And, sprinkled with parsley,
Serve you on toast."

Once again five little faces disappeared, ten little ears followed, and the loft was so quiet you could hear each of the he-cats breathing.

But kids must be kids and kittens must be kittens, and about the time the big cats fell asleep again, the kittens were climbing out of the box again and chasing their tails.

Polo expected Texas Jake to yowl and hiss and snarl, but this time the big cat simply climbed up in his rocker and began talking in a low, low voice:

"Once upon a time," he said, "there were five little kittens who lived in the loft with their mother. One afternoon the big cats wanted to take a nap, but the kittens weren't sleepy. 'Please go to sleep!' said their mother, but all the kittens replied, 'No, we're not sleepy.' So the big cats dozed off, and the kittens played. They scampered and skittered, they chattered and chased, they mewed and they meowed. And somewhere, far, far away, Bertram the Bad heard them. Bertram with his big sharp teeth; Bertram with his big strong legs; Bertram with his long pointy toenails."

The five little kittens sat transfixed, listening to the story, and Texas Jake continued:

"He came loping and lapping into the garage. He came

sniffing and snuffling up the stairs. He came creeping and crawling across the floor. He came slinking and sliding over to where the five little kittens were playing, and suddenly . . . GOTCHA!" Texas Jake yelled.

Five little bodies dived into the rag box.

Five little tails disappeared after them.

Not one of the kittens came out of the rag box the rest of the night.

But Polo didn't sleep. He stayed at his post just as he had promised he would, and early the next morning he heard a flopping and flapping outside the loft, a scritching and scratching on the sill, and suddenly the morning sun was blocked by a huge black crow, poking his head with his sharp yellow beak in through the loft window, and then hopping onto the floor.

Polo was there in an instant.

"What do you want?" he asked.

The other cats sprang to their feet also, and immediately encircled Carlotta and her kittens.

"Relax," said the crow. "I just came to see the new kittens. I thought I heard a mewing when I passed once by this window, and decided I would come and pay my respects."

"You will take none of these kittens with you!" Texas Jake told him. "The he-cats and I will fight to the death."

"Don't get your tails in a tangle," the crow said. "I just came to see if the young ones were hale and hearty, and offer to carry off any diseased or dying kitten among them."

At this Carlotta all but covered her brood with her body, but she needn't have bothered, for the crow took a brief turn around the loft, prancing on his slender sticklike legs, then gave her a quick nod.

"May your brood live a long and healthy life, ma'am," he said. "But if they don't, you can always call on me, your friendly neighborhood picker-upper, for I like them when the bodies are still warm. Adieu."

With that, the crow pranced back to the loft window, perched on the edge, and with one more glance at Carlotta and her kittens, he spread his shiny black wings and sailed out into the sky.

The he-cats stared helplessly after the crow, and then at each other. Bertram knew the kittens had come, Steak Knife and his Over the Hill gang had heard the news, and the crow had seen them with his own beady eyes. Yet nothing the members of the Club of Mysteries could do would make the kittens grow up any faster. All they could do was wait until Nature told them it was time.

Eight
A Visit to the Kiwanis Club

As the kittens grew bigger still, Carlotta's milk didn't seem to be enough for them. More and more they relied on the he-cats to bring them food from the Fishmonger.

One morning the kittens were particularly frisky, and by noon they were so hungry, and mewing so pitifully, that even Carlotta couldn't stand it.

"Please go to the Fishmonger and bring back whatever you can to feed my kittens," she begged the others. "They are exhausting me and driving me crazy."

Texas agreed to go on guard duty this time if Marco would bring him back a choice piece of salmon, so the others set out early to visit the Fishmonger, and were greatly disappointed to find that almost nothing had been thrown in the garbage cans yet.

"Well, this is a fine state of affairs!" said Elvis. "If we go back without any food, the kittens will drive *us* crazy!"

"Why do you suppose there is no one eating yet?

Could the restaurant be closed?" Polo wondered.

The cats crept over to a window, stood up on their hind legs, and peeked in.

Instead of lots of people enjoying their crab legs and French fries and flounder, however, there were fifty men in suits and ties, all sitting at long tables with their half-eaten lunches before them, listening to a man at the front of the room.

"Who do you suppose they are?" asked Boots. There was a sign on the wall, and all the cats looked at Marco.

"K-I-W-A-N-I-S," Marco said, spelling out the word, but he had no idea what it meant. "It's some kind of a club," he said, trying to figure it out.

"Perhaps they are hunters, and they go hunting Kiwanis, whatever they are," said Boots.

"Maybe they're sportsmen, and they play a game called Kiwanis," said Polo.

"Or cooks!" said Boots, hungrily. "Maybe they have cooked a Kiwanis and they are eating it."

Whatever it was, though, the men had stopped eating, and Polo wondered how men could sit so still for so long. Suddenly, to the cats' astonishment, the two-legged at the front of the room stopped speaking, and all the men began banging their hands together. It was the strangest thing the cats had ever seen, and it made a terrible racket.

Clap, clap, clap, clap, clap, clap, clap, clap.

"Why are they hitting their own paws?" Polo cried.

It was only one of many things the two-leggeds did that the cats could not understand, however, and while all the men were busy clapping their paws together, the cats crept in the back door, which had been propped open with a saucepan to cool the kitchen down.

Inside it smelled delicious, and just as the cats reached the dining room, flattening themselves along the wall in the hallway so as not to be noticed, the men in the dining room began to stand up and talk among themselves. And then they did another surprising thing. They extended their paws, grabbed hold of someone else's, and shook them up and down.

All over the dining room . . . *Shake, shake, shake, shake, shake, shake, shake.*

"I tell you," said Marco, "two-leggeds have got to be the strangest creatures that ever lived. They can open bottles, drive cars, build bridges, cook fish—they can do all sorts of things with their paws—but what are they doing? Standing in a room shaking their paws up and down."

The problem was, there would be no leftover food thrown into the garbage cans until the waiters could take away the plates. And the waiters did not seem to want to go in the room and begin removing plates until the men stopped shaking their paws and went home. The men did not appear to be leaving, and it seemed to the cats as though they would go on shaking paws forever.

"All right, enough!" whispered Marco. "Do you see that far corner, where the men are all standing around with their backs to the table? When I give the signal, we'll sneak in there and grab whatever is left on any of those plates. Try not to make a sound, or let the two-leggeds see you, and then head for the door."

With tails straight up in the air, one cat behind another, they marched forward again, and Marco gave the signal.

Carefully, carefully the four cats crept into the room, hopped up on the banquet table, grabbed the first thing they found, and while the members of the local Kiwanis Club went on talking loudly and shaking hands, they streaked back out again and down the hall. Only one man saw them, but he was too astonished to speak. By the time he nudged a companion, the cats were gone, and didn't stop running until they reached the loft.

The kittens began to tear into the food that the he-cats had brought. There was salmon and chicken and fillet of sole. The choice piece of salmon was reserved for Texas Jake, of course, but the kittens pounced on the rest as though it would get away, and Marco could tell that it wouldn't be long before the kittens and their appetites would be so big that it would take several trips a day to the Fishmonger to keep them happy.

Later, when Carlotta and her kittens were fast asleep, Texas called a meeting at the other end of the loft, and he kept his voice low.

"You can see for yourselves, lads, that this can't go on much longer. Tomorrow we must each start teaching the kittens a lesson. Winter is on its way out, and I feel the stirrings of spring. As long as the air was cold and there was snow on the ground, the kittens were content to stay in the loft in the rag box, but when birds begin to sing and bugs to crawl and grass to grow and rain to fall, they will want to be out, sniffing the big wide world. Their job is to learn at least one new thing each day. *Our* job is to be sure that five little kittens are accounted for when each of the lessons is over. And that may be far more difficult than you think."

Nine
A Lesson in the Fine Arts

When the kittens had nursed the next morning, Texas Jake ordered them to sit in a row and pay attention. There was no time now to waste. The sooner the kittens learned to survive for themselves, the better. Hamburger, Scamper, Mustard, Sugar, and Catnip went right on playing with their tails until Texas gave them a swat with his paw. *Then* they paid attention.

"Kittens," he said, "you may think that life is just a bowl of Chompies, but you are wrong."

"Wrong!" echoed the big cats.

"You may think that Carlotta will stay right here to feed you for the rest of your lives, and that all you have to do is eat, sleep, and chase your tails, but you are wrong."

"Wrong!" chorused the other cats again.

"No matter where you find yourselves, no matter how kind your master or mistress, you will need the skills we are about to teach you, because, my dear little kittens, you do *not* have nine lives, you have only one," Texas Jake continued.

The kittens had begun to grow restless again. Mustard, in fact, was nibbling on Carlotta's paw, and Texas leaned down and nipped him on the leg.

"Pay attention!" he thundered. "There are men who would drown you."

The kittens stopped wrestling and pricked up their ears.

"There are cars that would run over you," Texas said.

The kittens sat still.

"There are rats that would bite you, children who would tease you, and dogs that would tear you limb from limb."

The kittens began to shake.

"Tonight," said Texas, "we shall take you out for the very first time. But right now, Polo will teach you to leap."

"I can leap already," Catnip said, and jumped three inches off the floor.

"You must leap higher than that," Polo told them. "If you kittens are to save your skins, you must be prepared to jump ten times higher than that. Watch!"

Polo leaned back on his haunches, tensed his legs, and suddenly catapulted himself upward. He jumped from the cot to the back of the rocking chair, from the rocking chair to the lamp, from the lamp to a rafter, and back down to the floor again.

The kittens stared in amazement.

"And now, one by one," Polo instructed. He taught them to crouch, to tense their legs, and then to shove off with their muscular hindquarters.

Hamburger landed on his nose.

Scamper skidded across the floor.

Mustard collided with the lampstand.

Sugar sailed right over the army cot and tumbled down the other side.

While Catnip rose six inches in the air and came down again in the same spot.

But Polo patiently worked with each kitten until at last they were able to get up on the army cot and stay there, and that was enough for one day.

"When the weather is warmer," Texas Jake told them, "I will teach you to hunt. But for now, until the evening's adventure begins, we will teach you a thing or two about the fine arts. Elvis here will teach you to sing, for a cat without a yowl is hardly a cat at all. And Marco"—here Texas cast a disdainful look at the silver tabby—"will teach you to reeeaaaad, not that it's worth much to a cat who can see and hear and smell, but we might as well add it to the grocery list." And Texas promptly curled up in his rocker to take a nap.

Elvis climbed up on the army cot next.

"Do as I do," he said. He stretched out his neck and lifted his head. "Softly now," he began, "for we don't want the neighbors to hear. *Do, re, mi, fa, so, la, te, do,*" he sang, his voice rising a note at a time up the scale.

"*Mew, meow, mee, mi, mo,*" sang the kittens, such a cacophony of noise that Texas Jake startled, and the older cats wrinkled their noses and turned away.

Elvis had each cat try it one at a time. Sugar and Scamper and Mustard mastered it fairly well, but Hamburger and Catnip were hopeless.

"Never mind," said Elvis. "It will come. Just practice your fa's and your ti's, and we'll have a lesson again another day."

Then it was Marco's turn.

"The English alphabet has twenty-six letters," he told them. "Put together in different combinations, the letters spell words."

The kittens nodded their little heads.

"But sometimes," Marco went on, "two words can sound exactly the same, but are spelled and mean different things. Like *red,* as in color, and *read,* as in book."

"That's very confusing," said Scamper.

"And sometimes two words can be spelled exactly the same, but sound and mean different things, like *wind,* as in breeze, and *wind,* as in clock."

The kittens' eyes crossed in confusion.

"Never mind," said Marco hastily. "For now there are only two words you should know above everything else. B-e-w-a-r-e and d-o-g."

"This is too hard!" complained Catnip.

"This is too boring!" said Mustard.

"But if you can read, you'll be able to read stop signs!" said Marco.

"If it's red with white letters, we stop," said Elvis, not helping at all.

"But if you can read, you can read newspapers!" Marco protested.

"And learn about all the violence in the world?" asked Carlotta sadly. "Maybe it's better that they did not know how."

"But if you can read, you—"

"Can be the cat who can reeeeaaaaad!" growled Texas Jake, opening one eye. "Maybe one such cat in the Club of Mysteries is enough. I now declare the lesson to be over for the day."

Marco went back to his post at the top of the stairs

while Polo stretched out on a pile of newspapers for his morning nap. How sad, Marco thought, that for a cat who couldn't read, a newspaper was only good for lying upon or for doing one's business on in the litter box.

"Why is it," he asked his brother, "that the creatures who can read know of all there is yet to learn, and the creatures who can't read think they know all there is worth knowing?"

"I don't know, Marco," said his brother. "You were always the smartest of the litter. I can't even understand what you just said." And placing his head on his paws, he sank blissfully into a lovely dream.

Ten
Saving Your Skins

That night was the kittens' first venture out.

As lookouts and Guards of the Stairs, Marco and Polo went down first to check out the alley from one end to the other. Then the line of cats and kittens proceeded quietly down the stairs.

Marco had never seen the kittens' eyes so large.

Polo had never seen their ears more alert.

They jumped at the slightest sound, startled at the sight of a spider, and stared at Mr. Murphy's car as though it were a huge metal monster ready to chew them to pieces.

"That," said Boots, "is a car; cars can move; and when a car begins to move, you want to be as far away as possible."

"When this car goes out and comes back," Texas Jake instructed, "it will be warm. You must not jump up on its lap. You must not crawl up *under* its lap, no matter how cold the day might be. Because, kittens, if the car begins to move, you will go with it, never to be seen again."

"The only time you go in a car is when your master or mistress needs to take you to a vet, and then you will howl and carry on something terrible," said Boots.

"What's a vet?" asked Catnip.

"A two-legged in a white coat who will put a cold metal circle against your chest and listen to your heart," said Marco.

The kittens shuddered.

"A two-legged who squeezes your jaws open and peeks in your mouth," said Elvis.

"A two-legged who takes a sharp needle and sticks you in the leg," said Polo.

"A two-legged who takes a thermometer and puts it up your bottom," said Texas Jake.

The kittens all began to mew at once.

"Hush," said their mother. "There are even worse things than that." None of the kittens asked what.

They walked single file down the alley to the street in the gathering dusk, the kittens crouching fearfully behind the big cats as cars whizzed by in both directions.

"Remember this," said Boots. "If you are ever run over by a car, you will be nothing but a pancake there on the pavement. A flat cat is a stupid cat, because if you look both ways before you cross, this is not likely to happen."

"Listen carefully," said Marco. "There are two things you must never do. You must never cross the street and continue on down the alley on the other side, for down that alley is a field, and beyond that field is a woods, and beyond that woods is the city dump. Do you know who lives in the dump?"

The kittens shook their heads.

"The Over the Hill Gang," Polo told them. "And do you know who their leader is?"

Again the kittens did not know.

"Steak Knife," said Marco. "And do you know what Steak Knife does to little kittens?"

The kittens mewed pitifully, almost too frightened to listen.

"He cuts off their tails as trophies," Marco said.

"I want to go home!" wailed Catnip.

"Not yet," said Texas. "There's more." He led the line of cats and kittens down an alley. While the older cats walked along the fence tops, from house to house and yard to yard, Carlotta kept her kittens down below. Finally they came to a tall fence. And there on the back of the fence was a sign that said KEEP OUT.

"What does the sign say, Marco, O cat who can reeeeaaaad?" asked Texas.

"K-E-E-P, keep," said Marco. "O-U-T, out."

Texas Jake looked down at the kittens. "Over this fence is the home of Bertram the Bad. He is a dog so big he could put a whole kitten in his mouth. He is so bad that he would, if he could, have kitten pancakes for breakfast, kitten salad for lunch, and kitten pie for dinner. He is so loud that when he barks, your ears begin to ring; he is so heavy that when he moves, the earth shakes. Watch."

With the kittens trembling down below, Texas disappeared from view as he jumped down onto the roof of Bertram's doghouse on the other side and let out a mournful yowl.

Instantly the ground began to tremble, the fence to shake, and a noise like thunder filled the air. From the other side of the fence came a bark so loud, a growl so terrifying, that the kittens didn't even wait for their mother.

They rushed headlong back down the alley, around the corner, and didn't stop until they were once again safely up in the loft of Murphy's garage.

"Tonight you had your first lesson," Texas Jake told them. "Tell me something you have learned. Hamburger?"

"A car can eat a kitten in one gulp," Hamburger answered.

"No, no, no! That's Bertram," said Texas. "Sugar? What have you learned?"

"A flat cat is a sad cat," said Sugar.

"No, no, no! A flat cat is a dead cat," said Texas. "Mustard? Surely you must have learned something?"

"Never crawl under the hood of a sleeping car," said Mustard.

"Never crawl under the hood of *any* car, sleeping or not," said Texas. "Sometimes they stand perfectly still, purring loudly, and they are even more dangerous then. Scamper, what did you learn tonight?"

"Never go down the alley on the other side of the street without a steak knife," said Scamper.

"No, no, no!" cried Texas. "Never go down the alley on the other side at all, for Steak Knife and his gang are waiting. Catnip? Surely one of you kittens has learned something useful."

"The world is a very scary place," said Catnip.

"Right. Finally, right! Carlotta, is this the best you can do with your kittens?" Texas growled.

"Be kind, Texas, they are still young. You weren't so smart yourself at their age," Carlotta told him.

"But it's dangerous out there. They could be eaten alive."

"I know that," said Carlotta. "But a mother must learn to trust, and I trust that you and all the other members of the Club of Mysteries will protect my darlings until they are able to take care of themselves."

"We will try, Carlotta," the he-cats promised.

But Marco and Polo, as Guards of the Stairs, had seen the shadows in the alley, had heard the strange stirrings and rustlings and whispers and scurryings. They knew that the news of Carlotta's kittens was spreading far and wide, and that the kittens couldn't be left alone for even a minute.

Eleven
Bad News

It's time I went home and put in an appearance," Carlotta said one morning.

She had just nursed her kittens, and they were all lying lazily around, with milk on their jowls and tails in a tangle.

"My master hasn't seen me for over three weeks," she continued. "If I don't go back now and then, he might think I'm gone for good and give all my things away—my satin bed, my ceramic water dish, my toys, my fancy collars. . . . The kittens are all fed and napping, so if I can count on you gentlemen to watch over them, I'll be back in an hour or so."

"Of course you can count on us, Carlotta," said Marco.

"Nothing shall harm a hair of their heads," said Elvis.

So Carlotta leaned over the rag box to gently sniff each kitten, to tuck in a paw here and clean an ear there and lick around their mouths with her long pink tongue. And then, when she had finished, she crept quietly down the stairs.

The he-cats edged a little closer to the rag box, each wanting to show that he was the cat most in charge of kitty-sitting. But the kittens were indeed an awesome sight, with their small mouths and button noses, one head on another's stomach, or paw over an eye, or leg over a tail. Their bellies rose gently up and down as they slept.

"What do you suppose sleep is, anyway? That's a mystery I'd like to solve," said Polo after a while. "Why wouldn't lying down be enough?"

"Anyone knows that, Stupid," said Boots. "Every day cobwebs form in your mind, and sleep is like a broom cleaning your head."

"Oh," said Polo.

"That's not the reason," said Elvis. "Sleep is a way of making all your dreams come true. You can chase a mouse, catch a bird, escape a dog, and outrun a car. You can do anything at all in your dreams."

"Not me!" said Polo. "In *my* dreams the mouse chases me and the car runs right over my paw."

Marco tried to remember what he had read about sleep in the newspapers at the bottom of his litter box. But articles were often continued on another page, so if he started reading about one thing, he had to quit halfway through and read half an article on something else. Things got all mixed up together in his mind.

"I think that the brain is made up of neurons and protons," he ventured. "When you're awake, they all lean in different directions, but when you sleep, they line up perfectly like soldiers, ready to go. *This* is why you feel so alert when you first get up."

"Soldiers, schmoldiers!" cried Texas Jake, rolling his big

yellow eyes at the other cats. "Am I the only cat here who knows the Mystery of Sleep? Cobwebs! Neurons! Protons! Such nonsense! Sleep is to give the muscles in your neck a rest. If you did not sleep, they could no longer support your head. You would try to get up and your head would fall to one side. It would roll back and forth, a completely useless appendage to your body. Sleep is to hold your head on, lads, nothing more."

"Oh," said Polo again.

One of the kittens began to stir. His tail tickled the nose of another. The second kitten yawned and stretched.

"Oh, no! What do we do if they all wake up?" asked Boots warily.

"What if they all climb out of the box and start messing around?" said Elvis.

"What if they go downstairs?" said Marco.

"Sing to them, Elvis," Texas Jake commanded.

So Elvis sang:

"Sleep, kittens, sleep,
The river water's deep.
If you go out upon the town
You'll surely fall in and you'll drown,
Sleep, kittens, sleep."

Elvis had thought he would scare the kittens into going back to sleep, but he scared them awake, and all five kittens opened their eyes.

"Elvis, you numskull!" said Texas. "Sing them something peaceful, and hurry up."

Elvis tried again, but his second verse wasn't any better:

"Sleep, kittens, sleep.
You're tired little sheep.
If you crawl out we'll call the cops
Who'll turn you into tasty chops,
Sleep, kittens, sleep."

Now the kittens began to cry.

"You blubberhead! What kind of a singer are you? I thought you'd know a bedtime song," Texas thundered.

The four other cats of the Club of Mysteries put their heads together and finally came up with a different song, but they couldn't do much better than Elvis:

"Hush, little kittens, don't say a word,
Mama's going to bring you a tender bird.
If that bird don't taste too nice,
Mama's going to bring you a dish of mice.
If those mice crawl out the dish,
Mama's gonna bring you a smelly fish.
If that fish is just too rotten,
Mama's gonna—"

"Wah!" wailed the kittens. "We're hungry. We want our mama!"

At that moment Carlotta appeared at the top of the steps, and the kittens cried louder than ever, begging her to feed them.

"For heaven's sake," she said, climbing into the rag box and lying down so her kittens could nurse. "They were sleeping peacefully when I left. What happened? Can't five strong males entertain five helpless kittens for even half an hour?"

The he-cats looked sheepishly at each other.

"We tried!" said Boots.

"We sang to them!" said Elvis.

"But when one woke up, they all woke up," Polo tried to explain.

"I don't know how you do it, Carlotta," Marco told her. "It takes a mother's touch, I guess."

Now that the kittens were nursing again, gently kneading and pawing their mother's belly, the he-cats stretched out for a midday nap, all but Marco, who took his post at the top of the stairs. Then Carlotta's voice broke the stillness:

"I'm frightened!" she said, and suddenly all the cats paid attention.

"Why?" asked Texas. "What is it, Carlotta?"

"It's my master. I thought he would be glad to see me, and he was, I guess. He took out a bottle of cream and filled my bowl to the top. He petted my ears and smoothed my tail, but I heard him say to my mistress, 'She's had her kittens, all right. Now, where do you suppose they are?' And my mistress said, 'We've got to find them. She may have had them under someone's porch, and we can't have the neighbors complaining.' I *did* have them under a porch, but no one complained because then I brought them here."

"So?" said Texas. "What's the problem?"

"So then my master said, 'I'll look for them tomorrow. What do you want me to do with them?' and my mistress said, 'Everyone we know already has a pet. We'll just have to take them to the pound.'"

The he-cats shuddered because they knew what

happened if you went to the pound. If no one adopted you within a week, it was good-bye world, that was what.

Carlotta continued, "'Oh, I hate to do that,' my master said. And my mistress told him, 'Take them out in the country, then, and drop them off. Maybe a kind farmer will feed them.'" Carlotta began to weep.

All the he-cats gathered around, very much distressed to see their beautiful Carlotta so sad. They licked her ears and nudged her nose.

"Don't cry, Carlotta," Polo said. "We'll help you find homes for your kittens."

"Yeah?" said Texas Jake. "And just what do you suggest? If we each took a kitten home with us, our masters might decide to keep the kittens and throw *us* out."

But the other cats continued to reassure Carlotta, nuzzling her neck and rubbing her head, until at last her eyes became tiny slits and then they closed completely. But none of the he-cats slept. Now it wasn't just Bertram the Bad they had to worry about, or the crow, or the Over the Hill gang, but the master.

Twelve
Polite Inquiries

Texas Jake told the others that he would serve as Commander in Chief, King of the Alley, Lord of the Loft, Cat Supreme, *and* Guard of the Stairs if they would go out searching for a home for the kittens. So while Carlotta napped, Marco and Polo, Boots, and Elvis went out to make polite inquiries as to who might be in the market for a kitten—five of them, in fact. Boots and Elvis set off in one direction, Marco and Polo in another, and the first creature the tabbies spied was Timothy, the mouse.

Actually, they didn't so much spy him as catch him—Marco did, anyway. One minute the two cat brothers were passing a row of garbage cans, and the next minute Marco sprang forward and clutched a small gray mouse between his paws.

"Sorry," Marco said, releasing him immediately. "Just habit."

"I'd think you would have learned by now," Timothy said, brushing himself off and unwinding the kinks in his tail. "You don't have to love me, Marco, but you certainly shouldn't try to eat me."

"Just practicing," Marco said. "Actually, in a few more days—well, just about now, maybe—we are going to be providing some friends of ours with a hunting lesson. You wouldn't like to volunteer, would you?"

"For what? A hunter?" squeaked Timothy.

"Uh . . . the hunted," Marco told him. "Just a mouse to practice on."

"Are you crazy?" cried Timothy. "Would you like to volunteer to have Bertram the Bad chase you every day, grab you in his teeth, and swing you around like a rag doll? And don't give me that 'some friends of ours' bit. I get around. I know where Carlotta keeps her kittens."

"Okay," said Marco. "But we have to find homes for them or her master will take them out in the country and drop them off."

"Off of what?" asked Timothy hopefully. "The edge of a cliff?"

Marco and Polo looked at him in horror. "Just let them go. Let them fend for themselves or starve!" Polo said.

"I can think of worse fates to befall a cat," said Timothy.

"Think!" Polo begged. "Isn't there any house you know of that could use a good cat? What about the home you're in now?"

"Are you totally nuts?" asked Timothy. "Do you think I want a cat pouncing on me in the kitchen when all I want is a crumb from the table? A cat sniffing me out at night and eating my young? Not a chance."

"Well, so long then," said Marco. "Sorry to have bothered you."

"You're excused. You're not so bad for a cat," said Timothy.

Marco and Polo went on down the alley and soon came to the crow, pecking at the remains of a run-over squirrel.

Polo could scarcely watch.

"Good morning," cawed the crow in its raspy croak. "Would either of you care to join me for breakfast?"

Marco glanced down at the little piece of fur and bone, and his mouth felt dry. "No, thank you," he said. "We just wondered if, in all your travels, you happened to know of someone who might be looking for a kitten."

"Why, *I* could use a kitten," said the crow. "If Carlotta's lost one of her young, that is. A little sickly, is it?"

"No!" said Polo at once. "And it disgusts me that you could even think about eating a dying kitten."

"Hey, be glad I'm not an eagle. If I were an eagle, I would be looking for a tender kitten. A kitten with its eyes scarcely open whom I could carry high in the air in my sharp beak and then drop onto the pavement below. Like cracking the shell on a hard-boiled egg, if you will. Then I would fly down and enjoy my treat."

Marco and Polo gasped. "Have you no feelings?" Polo cried. "Have you no shame?"

"I *said* if I were an eagle," the crow reminded them. "I've no wish to bother Carlotta's kittens if they are alive and well, but remember that even eagles have a nest full of babies needing food. Every creature is entitled to eat, is it not? Now, if you will kindly step to one side, I'll finish my brunch."

The cats went on, feeling more discouraged by the minute.

"Look for signs," Polo told his brother. "Maybe people who want kittens put a sign in the window."

So Marco looked for signs. There were FOR SALE signs in windows of cars. There were RENT signs in windows of houses. A sign on a fence read, GIVEAWAYS: SIX BLACK-AND-WHITE KITTENS FREE! TAKE ONE! Marco and Polo hurried on by. No need to stop here.

They came at last to the Fishmonger, and discovered that Elvis and Boots had ended up here too, and they'd had no better luck finding a home for Carlotta's brood. When a cat can't think of anything else to do, there are only two choices left: eat or sleep. They were just about to jump up on a garbage can and see what tasty morsel might be awaiting them there when down the alley and into the parking lot came Carlotta, followed by Hamburger, Scamper, Mustard, Sugar, and Catnip.

"Carlotta!" cried Elvis. "Are you sure you know what you're doing? What if your master sees you and takes your kittens away?"

"I thought of that," Carlotta said, "but if two-leggeds never see my kittens, they will not know how adorable they are, and if masters don't know they're adorable, why would they ever want one?"

Texas Jake came up the alley then and joined them. "I tried to talk her out of it, lads, but she wouldn't listen," he said.

Hamburger, Scamper, Mustard, Sugar, and Catnip had already caught a whiff of the wonderful aroma of a Friday Night Fish Fry, and were heading right over to the back door of the Fishmonger as fast as their twenty little legs would carry them.

"Stop!" cried Texas Jake, in the loudest meow he could muster, and twenty little legs came to a halt. Texas maneuvered himself between the kittens and the door. "Don't ever, ever, *ever* go through that door," he told them. "Only grown-up cats can risk that. If *you* go through that door and enter the kitchen, you will never be seen again. A white panel truck will pull into the parking lot, up to the back door of the Fishmonger, and the chef will carry you out by the scruff of your neck. He will drop you in the back of the truck, the doors will close, and you will never see your mother again."

"But we're hungry," meowed Hamburger.

"We're starving," said Mustard.

"And we smell fish," cried Catnip.

"Then you must learn your manners and eat as the rest of us do," Texas instructed, wanting to be in command in front of Carlotta. "First of all, *sit.*"

It was hard for the kittens to concentrate on sitting when there were so many good things to be tasted, but the five of them sat down on their haunches.

"Do you see those garbage cans?" asked Texas.

"Yes," said the kittens.

"They are full of morsels of fish—flounder and perch and trout and salmon."

"Crab and sole and shrimp and lobster," put in Polo, his own mouth beginning to water.

"What you must learn to do is to jump up on the rim of a can, and push the lid over just enough to shove down inside," Texas told the kittens, "but *not* enough to shovel the lid off. If the chef hears the garbage-can lids hit the pavement, he'll be out in a second, dousing us all with the hose."

"Rule number two," said Marco, eager to get in the act and show *himself* in command in front of Carlotta. "The old and the feeble eat before you do. No matter how hungry you may be, the Abyssinian, and any other cat who looks a bit gray in the whiskers, a bit sagging in jowls and belly, is allowed to go first. Only when he emerges with his prize in his jaws may you try your luck in the can, and as soon as you have found your supper, you must crawl out and let another have your place."

Texas Jake hissed softly under his breath, for he did not like the reference to gray whiskers and sagging jowls. However, it *did* mean that he always got to eat first, so he merely swiped at Marco with one paw as he hopped up on one of the garbage cans.

The kittens waited patiently on the curb while Texas Jake, the Abyssinian, and the Siamese had their dinner, but as soon as those three cats came out of the trash can, Marco told the kittens to go ahead.

It took three tries for Hamburger to leap to the top of the can. Scamper leaped *too* high and sailed right over the rim, landing in a pile of coleslaw. Mustard collided with Sugar, who leaped at the same time, and Catnip never did get to the top of the can; the others had to toss down little morsels for him to eat on the pavement.

It was too much to ask that none of them knocked off a garbage-can lid, and finally one did. Hamburger had just found a fat chunk of salmon, and in his hurry to give it to Catnip, bumped into the lid, which sat askew on the rim. It tumbled to the concrete with a terrible clatter.

Instantly the cats scattered—some down the alley, some up on a wall, some to the left, some to the right, as

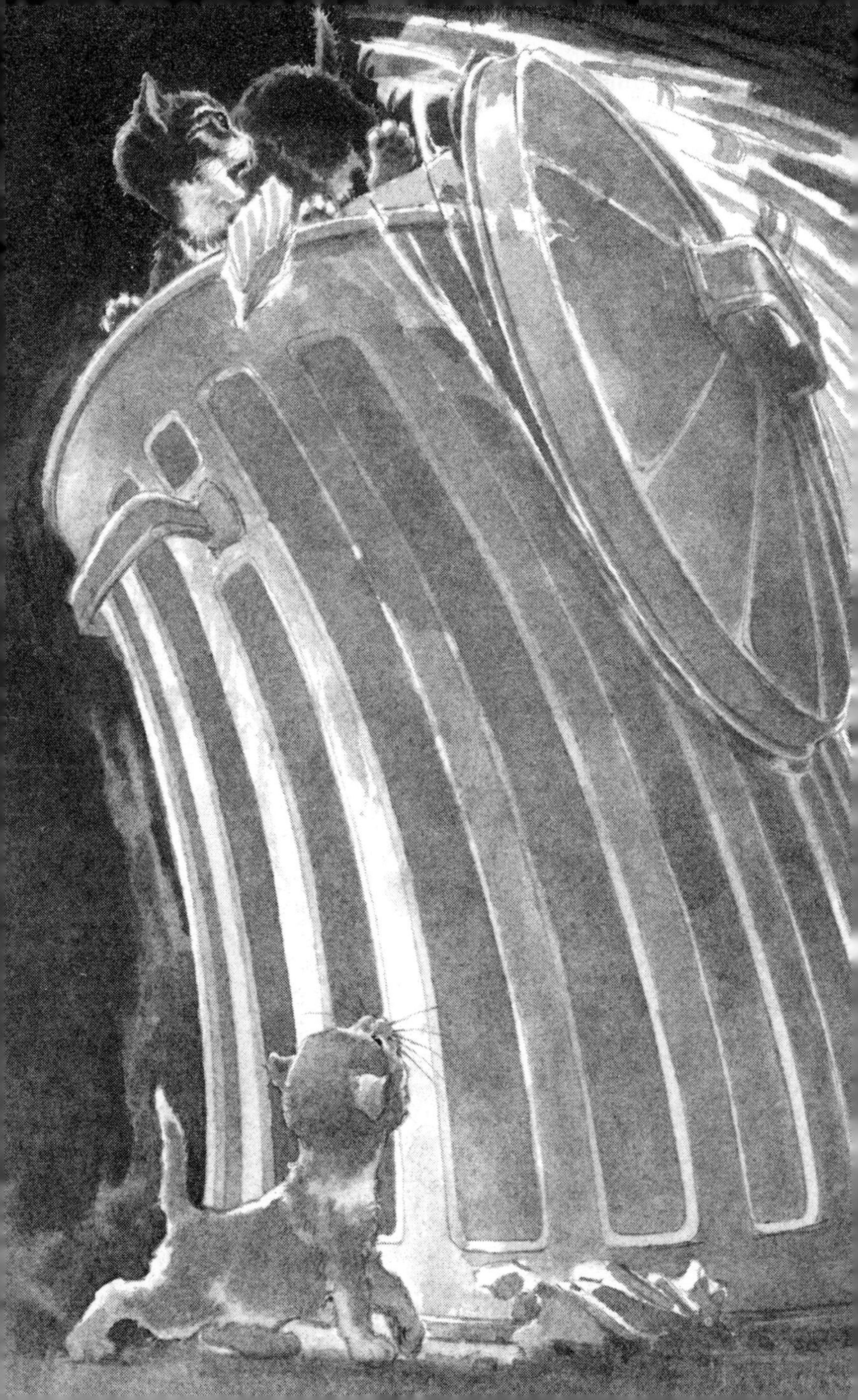

one of the chefs came out of the restaurant with a hose and sprayed the whole area. Seeing the piece of salmon there on the ground, he directed a stream of water toward it, and dozens of pairs of feline eyes watched in dismay as it floated along the gutter and disappeared down a storm drain.

But Polo had seen something else that upset him, he couldn't tell what. It was a shadow he hadn't noticed before, slinking along from doorway to doorway and disappearing as soon as Polo turned his head. There was a scent that was different from the other smells of the alley, and a certain clicking sound—long toenails, perhaps, that hadn't been trimmed in a dozen years. Whatever it was, whatever he sensed, Polo confided his fears to Marco, and when the kittens were safely back in the loft again, both tabbies decided to sit up that night and keep watch, just in case.

Thirteen
Walking the Line

Nothing happened that night, however, or the next, and so it was decided that the kittens were ready for another lesson.

Carlotta sighed. "If I'm going to be separated from my kittens—and mother cats are *always* separated from their kittens—then my babies must know how to live on their own. The greatest thing a mother can do for her kittens is to help them take care of themselves. The more I can teach them before they leave me, the better off they will be. And they, in turn, will be good to their own kittens when *they* become parents."

Her words were a tug at Polo's heart, for he, more than Marco, had memories of their mother. He didn't know what she looked like anymore, and he didn't know where she was, but whenever he thought of his mother, he thought of soft, warm, wiggle, purr, milk, tongue . . . and he missed that, whatever it was.

Had *she* helped him learn to survive? He really couldn't say, because most of what Polo had learned, he realized, he'd learned from his brother.

"Very well," said Texas. "We'll do whatever you think best, Carlotta. What do you want us to teach them next?"

"I want," said Carlotta, "to teach them to walk a straight line."

The he-cats stared. "Why should they need to do that?" Texas asked.

"If they can walk a straight line, they can keep their balance," said Carlotta. "And if they can keep their balance, they can walk along the top of the fence. And if they can walk the top of a fence, then I know they'll be safe, even if they are walking along the fence by Bertram the Bad."

Texas Jake drew himself up to his full height, thrust out his chest, and walked over to where the five kittens were sleeping, one on top of the other, in the rag box.

"At-ten-tion!" he barked, sounding more like a dog than a cat.

The five tiny kittens jumped, each opening one little eye, looked up at Texas, and promptly closed the eye again.

"On the *feet!*" Texas yelped.

This time the kittens opened both eyes, and when they saw the large yellow cat with the white belly staring down at them with his huge yellow eyes, they scrambled to their feet and fell over the side.

"Right . . . *face!*" Texas shouted.

The kittens, once they figured out which was right, made the turn.

"Left . . . *face!*" Texas thundered.

The kittens all turned to the left.

"For-ward, *march!*"

Scamper, who was second in line, bumped into Hamburger, who was supposed to be leading the way, and when Hamburger stumbled over his own paws, all the kittens ended up in a tumble on the floor.

"Did I say *at ease*?" Texas Jake boomed. "I don't *think* so!"

The kittens stood up again.

After he had marched them around and around the loft, Texas pointed to the long crack between two boards in the middle of the floor.

"Do you see that line?" he said to the kittens. "I want you to walk it. Don't step to the left; don't step to the right. Try to put all four paws on the line and see if you can walk from one end of the loft to the other."

Hamburger went first and promptly fell on his face. Scamper went next, and only slipped off the line once. Mustard was a bit wobbly, but he did okay, and by the time Sugar and Catnip walked the line, they had seen the other kittens try it and knew just how it should be done.

Carlotta sat down with her kittens.

"My dears," she said, "we are ready for one of the most important lessons of your life—we are going to walk the fence, and you must not, *must* not, lose your balance and fall, because if you do, you will fall into the yard of Bertram the Bad, who can tear you apart in one shake."

The kittens began to mew and tremble.

"We will walk five fences before we get to Bertram's," she continued. "Texas will go first, you will follow, and I will come along behind with the other cats."

"Keep your wits about you," said Marco.

"Watch where you put your paws," said Boots.

"Don't mew and meow," said Elvis.

"Keep your powder dry," said Polo.

Everyone looked at Polo.

"What's that supposed to mean?" said Texas.

"I don't know," said Polo. "It's just something you're supposed to say."

Off the cats went, tails in the air, Texas Jake first, followed by the kittens, and then Carlotta and the four other male members of the Club of Mysteries.

When they reached the end of the alley, Texas turned to the kittens. "Do you see that box?" he said. "Do you see that garbage can and that fence? I want each of you to jump up on the box, then the garbage can, and then the top of the fence. Follow me."

He crouched down on his haunches and jumped from box to trash can to fence. The kittens did as they were told. With much skidding and sliding, each managed to reach the top of the fence where they teetered back and forth, mewing pitifully.

With Carlotta following along behind, then the other cats, the procession began the long trek from one neighborhood fence to the next and the next, the big cats calling out their encouragement to the kittens.

As they neared the home of Bertram the Bad, Texas turned his large self around on the fence and faced the kittens: "This is it," he told them. "No more noise. Use your claws and hang on. Here we go."

The kittens were all trembling so violently that Polo, at the very end of the line, could feel the fence shake. Silently, stealthily, the six cats and five kittens made their way along the fence that separated Bertram the Bad's yard from the rest of the neighborhood. As they approached, Polo could see the roof of the doghouse, hear the snoring coming from inside, smell the odor of the huge mastiff who lay with one great paw sticking out the door of the doghouse along with the end of his majestic tail.

Perhaps he wasn't sleeping as soundly as they had thought, however. Perhaps he heard the squeak of the fence or smelled the aroma of tender young kittens. Because suddenly the noises stopped, followed by a snort, and then there was silence.

Polo had always thought there was nothing in the world as scary as Bertram the Bad's mighty roar. But now he discovered that silence was even scarier—the silence after a snore, when you can only dread what might be coming next.

Was the beast awake or asleep? Dreaming or listening? Were his muscles relaxing for another nap, or were they tensing, ready to spring?

It did not take long to find out, for suddenly the air was split by a roar so mighty that even Marco leaped. It was as though the earth beneath them had rocked and heaved. The fence shook and rattled. The huge beast leapt from the door of the doghouse, his mouth open wide, saliva dripping from the sharp edges of his long teeth.

The fur on the cats' and kittens' backs rose up so high they all appeared to be electrocuted, the pupils of their eyes grew large, and they stopped, frozen like statues, each with one paw in the air.

And in that moment of sheer terror, Hamburger let go, tumbled over the side, and into the yard of Bertram the Bad.

Fourteen

Rescue Number One

If cats don't have nine lives, they are at least good at thinking quickly in a crisis.

None of the big cats discussed what should be done, for instinct told them what each should do next.

While Carlotta urged her other kittens on until they were well past the yard of Bertram the Bad, Marco, Polo, Boots, and Elvis jumped down into the monster's yard and went streaking in one long line, like an arrow from a bow, across the length of the lawn.

Bertram, who was about to pounce on the terrified kitten, wheeled about when he saw not one, not two, not three, but four large cats invading his territory. He did a U-turn and went braying and thundering across the yard after them. In that instant Texas Jake hurled himself down into the mastiff's yard, grasped Hamburger by the scruff of the neck, and—with a great leap onto the roof of the doghouse and from there to the top

of the fence—carried him on to the safety of the other kittens.

Meanwhile Marco and Polo, Boots, and Elvis turned at the end of the yard and came racing back, jumping up onto the roof of the doghouse themselves, and from there to the fence, until at last all the cats, even Marco, who was fatter than a cat should be, were safe.

All the kittens did was cry. All they wanted to do was go home and cuddle up together in the rag box. Hamburger was still shaking. He wanted to snuggle down next to his mother and nurse. He wanted to feel her wet tongue on his head, to smell the scent of her soft body, and taste her warm milk.

But Carlotta said, "See? Do you see what can happen if you're not careful? What would you have done, Hamburger, if the other cats had not been there to rescue you? What will you do when you are out on your own? I will not always be around to look after you."

"Why?" asked Hamburger. "Where will you be?"

"Don't you love us?" asked Sugar. They had reached the garage, and the kittens followed their mother up the stairs to the loft.

"I love you now, and I will love you then. I love you here and I will love you there. I love you forever," Carlotta told them. "You will dream of me and I will dream of you, but in a little while you must find homes of your own." With that, she stepped into the rag box, lay down, and let her kittens nurse. Soon mother and kittens were sleeping.

The other cats began to get drowsy too, and their eyes formed little slits. But just as they were dozing off, recovering from their adventure, Polo asked, "Why?"

Texas opened one eye. "Why what?"

"*Why* can't our mothers be with us always? Why can't cats go out into the world and have an adventure and come home at night and snuggle up against soft, warm, wiggle, purr, milk, tongue?"

The cats tried to think why not.

"Because we grow too big to nurse?" Boots offered.

"That's right," said Texas Jake.

"And because the kittens themselves will be mothers and fathers someday?" suggested Elvis.

"True," said Texas Jake.

"And perhaps . . . because someday . . . when they are old . . . mothers die, and are no longer around to take care of us?" said Boots.

"That's a fact," Texas answered.

Marco agreed. "Nothing lives forever. Not cats or dogs or people or flowers or trees or stars—"

"Stars?" cried Texas. "That's ridiculous."

"No, it's true," Marco told him. "Even stars die after a long, long time, but you still see their light from millions of years ago. They are so far away that it takes a long, long time for their light to get to us."

"I never heard of anything so stupid!" said Texas. "If you see something, then obviously it is there."

Marco did not know enough about astronomy to argue with the big cat, and so he said nothing.

Once more the cats' eyes began to close, and when they were almost asleep again, Polo asked, "Why?"

"Why *what?*" Texas demanded, a little impatient now.

"Why doesn't anything live forever? If I have to die, then I'm sorry I was born a cat."

"Well," said Texas, "what would you rather be? A rock? Rocks don't die."

"Or a doorknob?" said Boots.

"A supper dish?" suggested Elvis.

"The only things that don't die are things that are dead to begin with, and you'd hardly want to be *them*," Marco explained.

Polo thought it over. No, he would not like to be a rock or a doorknob or a supper dish, for they had no fun at all. He closed his eyes and began to drift off to sleep.

"Why?" came a voice again, but it wasn't Polo's.

All the cats opened their eyes, because this time it was Texas Jake who had asked the question. "Why," he asked, suddenly sitting up, "does it take the light from the stars millions of years to get to us?"

"Because they are so far away," said Marco.

"But . . . but . . . *that* would mean," said Texas, "that when we look up at the sky at night, we don't know which of the stars are alive and which are dead!"

"Exactly," Marco told him.

"So we could be looking at ghosts of stars?" asked Boots.

"You could call it that," said Marco.

"Then the sky is full of ghosts!" cried Polo.

At this point, Carlotta and the kittens awoke, and the kittens all began mewing.

"Now see what you've done," Carlotta scolded the older cats. "I was all set to have myself a nice nap."

The he-cats began to apologize, but Carlotta climbed out of the rag box. "Now that you've wakened them, they're yours for the next couple of hours," she said. And to her kittens she added, "These nice cats will look after you for a while. Get ready for another adventure."

"What are we going to do this time?" asked Mustard. "What are they going to teach us now?"

Carlotta looked at the he-cats and then at her kittens.

"To hunt," she said, and left the loft.

Fifteen

On the Prowl

Texas Jake had no choice, and the five little kittens followed him down the stairs to the alley. They did not, however, stand still.

They squirmed.

They rolled.

They jumped.

They danced.

They wiggled, skidded, whirled, and pranced.

Scamper, in fact, pounced on Texas Jake's tail and must have thought they were playing Crack the Whip, because he wouldn't let go. Texas lashed his tail back and forth, back and forth, but Scamper held on and went whirling around like a mop.

"Stop!" Texas yowled, and the kitten let go. She went tumbling down the alley and would have crashed into a garbage can had Marco not stopped her with his paw.

"Now, listen up!" Texas ordered. His yellow eyes went

from one kitten to the next. "Your mother would like for me to teach you to hunt."

"What is 'hunt'?" asked Mustard.

Texas Jake stared. "What is hunt? You don't know what it is to *hunt*?" He looked at Marco, Polo, Boots, and Elvis.

"To hunt is to catch," said Polo.

"Catch what?" asked Hamburger.

"Anything that moves," said Boots.

"Anything that slithers, creeps, crawls, runs, flies, or swims," Texas instructed, swishing his tail. The kittens immediately pounced on it. "*Except* my tail," he thundered. "Anything that slides, glides, oozes, or wallows."

"Bugs, slugs, worms, crickets, beetles, flies, spiders, and mice," said Boots. "Especially mice."

But Hamburger still wasn't satisfied. "*Why* do we hunt things?" he asked.

"Why? *Why?*" Texas said. "Because they are there. Plain and simple."

"And what do we do after we catch them?" asked Catnip.

"Why, eat them, of course!" said Texas Jake.

"Oh, gross!" cried Catnip.

"Horrible!" said Mustard.

"You may think so," said Texas, "Indeed you may. But sometime you may be out in the world on your own. You may be hungry and cold, with nothing in your food dish and no place to lay your head. And if that ever happens to you, you'd better know how to hunt."

Frightened, the kittens paid attention.

"Now, watch," said Texas.

The kittens watched as Texas tensed his muscles,

bent his legs, lowered his belly, and twitched his tail.

"This is the crouch position," said Texas. "Most of the time, you do this *after* you see something you want to catch. But . . . " All at once his body stiffened even more, his tail began to swish harder, the pupils of his eyes grew larger, and . . . POUNCE!

A terrified squeal pierced the air.

"Timothy!" cried Polo, when he recognized his little friend fast in the clutches of Texas Jake. "Don't hurt him, Texas!"

"This is a Timothy?" growled Texas. "It looks like a mouse to me."

"He's our friend," said Marco, "and we're sworn to protect him."

Texas Jake tipped his head to one side and reconsidered. Finally he said, "All right, if he will let me use him for demonstration purposes, without claws, of course."

"Okay, Timothy?" asked Polo.

The tiny mouse could only swallow and nod his head.

Texas held out his paws so the kittens could see the way he was holding the frightened little rodent. "Do you see how I have him clamped securely between my paws?" he asked. "If this were for real—if Timothy were actually dinner—and if I thought he might get away, I would pin him in place like this." Texas extended eighteen long claws, and Timothy let out a squeal of fright.

"Each of these claws," Texas said, "would impale this succulent mouse, with no chance of escape whatsoever."

Squeak! went Timothy.

"But because this dainty succulent delicious scrumptious morsel has a name, because this tiny tender delicacy is

a friend to our tabbies here, I, out of the generous goodness of my heart, will let him go."

At that Texas Jake retracted his claws, opened his paws, and the mouse named Timothy disappeared like a streak of lightning.

"Now!" said Texas, rising to his full height once again in front of the kittens. "Assume the crouch position."

Hamburger lowered his belly but not his rump.

Scamper lowered his rump but not his belly.

Mustard went down on his nose.

Sugar sat down on her tail.

And Catnip was facing the wrong way entirely.

"You are sorry excuses for cats if I ever saw them!" Texas Jake declared. "All together now! Try again!"

The kittens bumped and rolled and turned and twisted, but finally, with a little coaching from Marco and Polo and

Boots and Elvis, they lined themselves up and assumed the crouch position.

"Now," said Texas, "keep your bellies low to the ground and follow me. But if you see something to catch, pounce!"

Slowly, slowly, step by step, the line moved forward down the alley.

Pounce!

Scamper saw a worm in an early March puddle nearby and retrieved it with one paw, then picked it up in his mouth and went parading grandly around in circles, showing off his prize.

"Well done!" said Texas. "Except that anyone can catch a worm. You could be blind and deaf and three-legged and still catch a worm. You could sit in a puddle with your eyes closed and the worm would come to you! You don't get any points for catching a worm."

"Go easy on them, Texas. At least it was a good try," said Marco.

Pounce!

A second kitten made a catch. Mustard got a bug. It was a brown and orange bug that twitched and quivered. When it tried to fly away, Mustard pressed it tightly between his paws.

"What did you get?" asked Boots, coming over to see.

Mustard spread his paws just a little. Then he spread them wider still. "Where did it go?" he asked, puzzled. All that was left was a spot. A smudge. A little glob of brown and orange.

"Eee-yuk!" cried Catnip.

"That's life," said Elvis. "*Was* life, anyway."

"Onward!" Texas said, and the hunting party started off again, bellies low to the ground.

The next catch was more like a show, for Hamburger found a beetle, and everyone stopped to watch. He did not catch the beetle as much as the beetle caught him. It snapped at him and pinched his nose. In fact, it wouldn't let go.

Mewing loudly, Hamburger ran around and around in circles, the beetle making clicking sounds, until finally Texas Jake came over, swatted at the beetle with one large paw, and then snapped it up in his jaws.

Crunch, munch, crackle, pop!

"Oooh!" cried the kittens.

But it was Catnip's turn next. As they prowled through an old garage, a large hairy spider dangled in front of them, a tempting treat.

Catnip tried to catch the spider, but it scurried up to the top of its web. Catnip stood on his hind feet and batted at the web. It stuck to his paw, and the more he waved his paw, the more web he wrapped around it, like a stick of cotton candy.

"Help!" cried Catnip, trying to rub the web off on his ear, but now his ear was covered too, and soon there was web on his nose as well. The spider didn't make a sound, but seemed to be laughing at him from his perch in the air.

The other kittens came to help.

Soon they all had webbing on their paws, and the spider crawled away, just out of reach.

"So who wanted a spider anyway?" said Catnip.

It was right at that moment that Hamburger saw the bird.

It was a small black-and-white chickadee that flew into the old garage, up into the rafters, and then swooped low again and out the door.

"Now, that," said Texas, "is the most difficult lunch of all."

The kittens crouched low on the floor of the garage watching the chickadee swoop in and swoop out, in and out. Their heads went up, their heads went down, up and down, up and down, and the first thing anyone knew, all five kittens had nodded off to sleep.

"The great hunters," said Marco fondly, looking at the soft little heads snoozing so peacefully.

"Not a care in the world," said Polo.

"They hardly know anything about life on the outside," said Elvis.

"All they care about is getting back home to their mother," said Boots.

The big cats were quiet for some time, each one, perhaps, remembering when *he* had been a little kitten and knew nothing about the dangers of the world beyond.

Finally Texas sighed.

"Well, kittens," he said, "Let's call it a day. Let's pack it in." He went along the row, nudging each kitten, until all five were awake now. And then, tired from their adventure and hoping for their mother's milk, they rose up on their feet and followed Texas back to the loft in Murphy's garage, unmindful of what would happen next.

When they reached the top of the steps, Carlotta was already there. She had used the time to return and take a nap, and sleepily rolled over on her side to feed her kittens. Hamburger jumped into the box first, followed by Mustard and Scamper and Sugar and . . .

The big cats looked around. Carlotta sat up and meowed. All her kittens were there except one. Catnip was missing.

Sixteen
Into the Pipes

Never mind the other kittens.

Carlotta jumped out of the rag box.

"Where's little Catnip?" she asked. "What has happened to him?"

The big cats stared at each other.

"Do you mean to tell me that five grown cats could not take care of five little kittens for one afternoon?" Carlotta asked.

"But . . . he was just here, Carlotta! I mean, he was right out there in the alley," said Texas Jake.

There was skittering and scuttling on the stairs, and all the cats turned to see the little mouse Timothy come to a skidding stop on the floor of the loft.

He must be one brave little mouse to enter a room with six cats and four kittens! thought Polo, as he saw some of the cats hunker down in the crouch position, ready to spring.

But the little mouse was taking no chances. He scurried

up one of the posts to the rafters and then he squeaked, "One of the kittens was taken! They took him away!"

"Who?" cried Carlotta. "Who has my kitten?"

"The rats. The river rats. I saw them hiding behind the garbage cans, and when the rest of you went by, they grabbed the kitten on the end."

Carlotta collapsed on the floor, her four remaining kittens mewing fearfully around her.

"Boots," said Texas Jake, "stay here and look after her. Elvis, guard the door in case the rats come back for the rest. If Marco and Polo will come with me, we will look for Catnip."

Marco and Polo were astonished that Texas Jake had chosen them. Boots and Elvis had been members of the Club of Mysteries long before the tabbies had joined. But he and his brother wanted to prove to both the big cat and Carlotta that they were courageous, and would do whatever was necessary to get little Catnip back.

"Thank you, Timothy," Texas said, and looking around the loft, added, "Let it hereby be known that none of us should ever eat that mouse."

"Or my wife and children," said Timothy.

"Or his wife and children," said Texas Jake. "If we catch them by mistake, we shall let them go."

"I'm surely glad to hear that," squeaked Timothy, much relieved.

"Do you know where they took him? Where do the rats hang out?" Texas asked him.

"They live in the sewer," said Timothy. "Down by the river. And they're a mean, mean bunch, those rats."

Carlotta moaned again.

"Carlotta," said Marco, "we will do everything we can to get your kitten back. I promise."

"*We* promise," Texas Jake corrected him. And with that, he went down the stairs, Marco and Polo behind him, and out into the gathering dusk.

"What would the river rats want with a little kitten?" asked Polo. "He's hardly strong enough to do anything for them."

"Except provide a tender meal," said Texas Jake. "I only hope we're not too late."

Marco and Polo knew something that Texas did not—they knew how to get down into the sewer and where the sewer led, for a few months back, when Texas Jake had asked them to solve the mystery of where water went when it rained, they had climbed down into a storm sewer and met the rats there. That was why Texas wanted them along.

So with Marco and Polo leading the way this time, they went down the street to the storm sewer at the corner and—one by one—crawled down into the opening beneath the street.

It was dark in the tunnel. It was cold and wet. And when they spoke, the cats' voices echoed along the pipes.

"Where do we go now?" whispered Texas, and the tunnel was filled with *now, now, now, now, now. . . .* Marco realized that this was the first time the big cat, Commander in Chief, Lord of the Loft, King of the Alley, Cat Supreme, had ever asked his opinion—ever acknowledged he needed help.

"We follow it west toward the river," Marco answered. "As we go, we will begin to hear murmurs. We will see the gleam of eyes peering out at us from side tunnels. And then we will begin to feel the vibration of paw-steps along the pipe—softly at first, then louder and louder as the rats begin to run, and soon there will be hordes of them all around us. And *then* it will be up to you, Texas, as to what we do next."

Polo was shaking too badly to say anything himself. He remembered what had happened before when he and Marco were in the sewer together, following the tunnel to see where it would lead, just so they could go back and tell the others where water went when it rained. He remembered how the rats had chased them, and the tabbies had ended up half drowned in the river.

This, however, was different. This was for Carlotta's kitten, the smallest, the runt of the litter. Polo's biggest fear was not of what might happen to him and Marco and, least of all, to Texas Jake, but that they might be too late to save Catnip. For, being the smallest kitten of the litter, he was probably also the most tender.

A narrow stream of water ran down the center of the tunnel, the runoff from the last rain, and from far, far away, like a distant waterfall, the cats could hear the sound of the stream as it tumbled into the river. There were pipes all along the tunnel—pipes here, pipes there, and all the little trickles of water together would grow and grow until finally there would be a virtual torrent emptying into the river at the end.

Texas Jake was not as young as Marco and Polo, and because of his fight once with Bertram the Bad, he had battle scars to show for it. He walked with a limp, and while the two tabbies were limber enough to dodge a sudden gush of water from a drainpipe, Texas was not, and he was beginning to get quite wet.

A wet cat, as everyone knows, is a cross cat, and Texas was not enjoying this adventure one bit.

And then, just as Marco had said, the whispers began—so soft at first they were hard to distinguish.

"Look!" the whispers went, and then the echo, *look, look, look, look, look* . . . echoing on and on.

A pair of beady eyes gleamed here, more eyes there—two eyes, four eyes, six eyes, eight. . . . The eyes were multiplying, the whispers becoming louder, until suddenly an army of rats seemed to be coming down the sewer toward them.

Polo's first impulse was to run, but the cats hadn't come to be chased, and Texas Jake turned at once to face them.

There is something about a cat, an old cat, a Commander in Chief, Lord of the Loft, King of the Alley, and Cat Supreme, that commands respect even among his mortal enemies. There is something about such a cat turning and facing his attackers that made the rats skid to a stop.

"Who goes there?" came the raspy voice of the Rat Commander.

And Texas answered in turn, "Texas Jake goes here, with Marco and Polo. We've come for Carlotta's kitten."

"What makes you think we would kidnap a kitten?" asked the Rat Commander.

To which Texas Jake replied, "Only you can answer that, Commander, but where is Catnip?"

"Gone," said the Rat Commander, and the walls of the tunnel echoed his answer: *Gone, gone, gone, gone, gone*. . . .

Polo felt his legs almost give way. Marco's heart seemed to stop in his chest.

"Gone where?" asked Texas Jake.

"To the boss," answered the rat.

"What boss? I thought you were the boss of the sewer," said Marco.

"The sewer, yes, but I'm talking about the Lord of the Dump," said the rat.

Polo gasped in horror. "Steak Knife?"

"He's the one," said the Rat Commander.

"But why?" asked Texas.

"Who knows?" said the rat, and his answer echoed, *Knows, knows, knows, knows, knows. . . .*

"Why would you work for him?" asked Marco.

"An even exchange, you might say," said the rat. "When we can do a favor for Steak Knife, he allows us a day at the dump. And there's nothing a rat likes better, as you can imagine. A day at the dump, with no cat on our tails, so to speak."

It was the way he said it that made Marco's blood run cold. He suddenly remembered that Steak Knife had a collection of tails—rat tails, cat tails, dog tails, racoon tails, mouse tails. . . .

"Texas, we don't have a moment to waste," said Marco. "Catnip is about to lose his tail, and possibly his life as well."

“Make way!” thundered Texas Jake, and the rats parted, making a path through the throng, so that Texas and Marco and Polo went back the way they had come, knowing that every second might be a second too late for Catnip.

Seventeen
Steak Knife's Collection

Why did it seem longer to get out of the sewer than it did to get in? Polo wondered. He could hear Texas panting behind him, and Marco, who was fat, followed last. Yet it was the first time Polo could remember that *he* had been a leader in the Club of Mysteries. That Texas Jake followed *him.* Depended on him. Polo was quick and lean, and knew all the twists and turns they had taken following the tunnels to find the rats.

Now he was the first one to hop out of the storm sewer when they finally reached the street, and it was he who led the way back up the street to the Fishmonger, then across to the alley on the other side.

For the first time either of the tabbies could remember, Texas Jake treated them as equals. On this quest for Carlotta's kitten, he did not make fun of them, did not tell Polo he was stupid, did not call Marco "the cat who can reeeeeaaaaad. . . . " He was as sober as the tabby brothers had ever seen him, and both Marco and Polo knew there was but one thing on his mind: little Catnip.

The alley became a dirt lane, the lane became a path, the path led into a field, and night was beginning to fall. In this twilight zone between light and dark, things seemed to stand out more clearly on the land, shapes more distinct, colors more vivid. As they crossed the field, the black crow swooped down and flew overhead.

"Do you know where you are going?" he cawed. "You are heading for Steak Knife's lair. Beware! Beware!"

"We know," said Marco.

"And his Over the Hill gang," continued the crow. "Caw caw! Caw caw!"

"We know that too," said Polo. "But he has the littlest of Carlotta's kittens, and we have to get him back."

"Caw. Caw. Good luck! Good luck!" the crow called, and flew high into the air again, until he was only a tiny black speck against the sky.

When they entered the woods—just as it had been in the sewers—there were whispers. They came from trees, from bushes, from behind rocks, out of hollow stumps and deep dark holes in the forest:

> *CATS, cats, cats, cats, cats, cats . . .*
> *TEXAS JAKE, Jake, Jake, Jake, Jake, Jake . . .*
> *SPIES, spies, spies, spies, spies, spies . . .*

"What do we do now?" asked Texas. "Where do we go?" For he himself had never tried to find the Over the Hill gang.

"Keep walking," said Marco. "The dump is through the woods, up the hill, and down the other side."

Well, thought Polo, even if they didn't survive, at least Boots and Elvis would be left to look after Carlotta and her kittens, to see that they found good homes. But why couldn't it have been Marco and Polo who had been left to care for them? What a happy life that would have been then! Marco, Polo, and Carlotta—forever and ever. Marco, Polo, Carlotta, Hamburger, Scamper, Mustard, Sugar, and Catnip, to be exact. Well, maybe not Catnip . . .

The sky was not quite dark, but the woods made it seem like midnight. The farther they went, the darker it became, and the darker it was, the more eyes appeared around them.

Texas Jake's footsteps had slowed, and the tabby brothers were more conscious now than ever of how old the big yellow cat really was. When he had rescued Hamburger from Bertram, it was easy to think of Texas Jake as young and strong. But after a long trek through the sewers, and now to the dump, his age was beginning to tell. Yet he never complained about his lame leg, never asked them to stop so he could rest. He wasn't Lord of the Loft, Commander in Chief, King of the Alley, Cat Supreme for nothing.

Whispers became hisses, hisses became words, words became sentences, and the sentences questions. And finally, just as Polo, who was in the lead, emerged from the woods and started up the hill toward the dump, two raggedy, scraggly cats appeared on either side of him like sentries and demanded, "Where do you think you're going?"

"We are looking for Steak Knife," Polo answered, as brave as he'd ever been.

A hiss seemed to fill the air, and traveled from tree to tree, bush to bush, log to log: *SSSSTEAK KNIFE, ssssteak knife, ssssteak knife, ssssteak knife, ssssteak knife, ssssteak knife. . . .*

"What is your business?" asked one of the cats, an ornery-looking cat with brown and white stripes, and half an ear missing. "Not just anyone can see him, you know."

"That is between him and us," spoke up Texas Jake, eager to reassert his authority. "Take us to him, lad, and be quick about it."

The cat with half an ear missing did not look like a lad to Polo, but no one had ever spoken to the striped cat in just such a way, so after a brief conference with the other guard of the dump, he said, "Follow us," and led the way.

Marco and Polo could smell the dump before they ever reached the top of the hill. They could smell rubber burning, garbage rotting, wood decaying, and other unpleasant odors. And when they started down the hill on the other side, they saw the most horrible sight of all—little Catnip, lying with his face in the dirt, held in place by the scruff of his neck by a huge reddish cat with one eye.

And suddenly, from over a pile of boxes and cans and tires and banana peels, stepped the roughest, toughest, mangiest, scraggliest, dirtiest cat that Marco and Polo had ever seen, and they recognized him at once as Steak Knife.

Seeing Marco and Polo and Texas Jake, little Catnip began to mew desperately, but the big red cat silenced him with one swift cuff to the head.

"You came to see me?" asked Steak Knife in a voice that had the sound of gravel sliding along a tin chute. And he looked down on them from the pile of junk, then made

his way through the garbage and landed silently on the ground between them.

Everything about the mangy cat reeked of battle—his scars, his cuts, his scrapes. One eye drooped, one ear flopped, one paw limped, and his tail was crooked. But there was no doubt at all that even the rats respected him for what he was: Lord of the Dump.

"We have come for Catnip, to return him to his mother," answered Texas Jake.

At this Steak Knife sneered. "I finally got my prize, and you came to take it away?"

"What prize is that?" asked Texas Jake.

Steak Knife led them over to the chain-link fence, and Polo's blood ran cold, for he knew very well, from his previous trip here, what was on that fence.

When Texas saw it, even he sucked in his breath, Marco noticed, for there was a hideous display of tails: rat tails, cat tails, mouse tails, dog tails, raccoon tails, bird tails, and even, they noticed, the tail of a skunk.

"I have every treasure but one . . . every cat tail you can think of—Persian, tabby, Abyssinian, Siamese—but I don't have the tiny tail of a kitten. And so," Steak Knife said with a terrible smile, "the rats obliged me."

"And for that they get a free day at the dump?" said Texas, his voice more a growl. His ears were laid back, his fur was beginning to rise, and Marco saw, to his horror, that he was preparing to do battle. Didn't he know there were many more cats hiding here in the dump who, if Texas attacked their master, would be on him in two seconds flat and tear him to shreds? That his own tail would be a trophy there on the chain-link fence?

"Give me the kitten," Texas demanded.

"Indeed!" said Steak Knife, beginning to smile. "You shall have him, sir, or what is left of him, as soon as we chew off his tail."

"No!" cried Polo.

Little Catnip mewed again.

Already the other cats were beginning to gather—a dozen or more scraggly, mangy, scar-faced cats, as used to fighting as they were to breathing. Marco knew there must be another way, and suddenly he stepped forward.

"Really, Steak Knife," he said, "your collection is much too valuable to ruin."

Steak Knife, whose own fur was beginning to rise, and who was facing off with Texas Jake, stopped and looked at him. "What do you mean?"

"I mean that you have tails of the most magnificent creatures. Anyone who viewed your collection would wonder to himself, 'How did he manage to get *that* one, or *that* or *that*? Surely he must have put up a terrible fight!'"

"Indeed I did!" said Steak Knife, pleased at the flattery.

"Such a collection is one of a kind. There is none like it in the world!" Marco continued, while Polo and Texas Jake stared.

"But," Marco continued, "if you were to add this tiny little tail of a kitten—a *kitten*—you would be the laughingstock of cats everywhere. What courage does it take to capture a kitty? Who could not get a tail of a defenseless kitten? Why, even a mouse could do it."

Steak Knife looked about him in surprise. He could see by the other cats' faces that they too had not considered this before. There surely was no honor in that.

"You are much too great a leader to stoop to this—to defame your magnificent collection with the scrawny little tail of Catnip."

"You seem to know a fine collection when you see one," Steak Knife said at last.

"Why, this collection is unique!" said Marco. "Cats would come from all over the city to see a display such as this."

"Well, perhaps you are right," said Steak Knife at last. "It was an idea, only an idea, but the collection is much too valuable for that." He turned to the red cat: "Release him," he said.

Hesitantly the red cat lifted his paws, and little Catnip scrambled shakily to his feet. With the kitten between them, Polo and Texas Jake started up the hill again, and Marco bid the Over the Hill Gang adieu. He said scarcely a word as they hurried along, but once they had made it through the woods and were starting to cross the field, Marco could hear distant shouts behind them.

"Trickery! Trickery! I have been tricked!" came the voice of Steak Knife, and the sound of running cat feet grew louder and louder.

"Run!" Texas Jake commanded. "I will never make it to the street, but you two must take Catnip back to his mother. I will stay and fight as long as there is breath in my body. Run! Run!"

"We can't leave you here," said Marco.

"Do as I say!" Texas Jake commanded, turning to face the Over the Hill gang who were racing out of the woods now and along the open path in the field. Steak Knife was in the lead with the reddish, one-eyed cat beside him, followed by the rest of the motley crew.

At that moment there was another sound, a *caw, caw* from overhead, and suddenly, out of the sky, came the black crow. Like a fighter plane, it dived at the Over the Hill gang, this way, that way, sending the scraggly batch running for cover.

As Marco and Polo and Texas Jake rushed on with little Catnip, they looked back to see the mangy cats scattering in all directions as the crow dive-bombed them again and again. It swooped over Steak Knife. It pecked at the cat with half an ear. It zigged and zagged and cawed and pecked, until finally the Over the Hill gang turned and tore back to the safety of the woods, and Catnip was safe.

Eighteen
A Little Disguise

Carlotta was so glad to see Catnip that she just about knocked him down, she licked him so hard.

"My littlest one," she meowed. "My Catnip."

The other kittens almost wished that *they* had been the one the rats had captured. Finally, when Carlotta was convinced that Catnip still had all his parts, tail included, she lay down and her grateful kittens swarmed over her, pushing and kneading and squealing with pleasure as they filled their tummies with warm milk.

"Tell me the whole story," Carlotta said. "How did you find the Rat Commander?"

Somehow the story sounded very different when Texas Jake told it: "If I had not known how to get down into the sewers and find him," he said, "Catnip never would have kept his tail."

"Ahem," said Polo.

"Of course, Polo helped," the big yellow cat admitted.

"For an inexperienced cat, he is quite agile, so it was good that I thought to take him along. But when we found Steak Knife and he was all ready to bite off Catnip's tail, only by my forceful persuasion did he agree to let your kitten go."

"Ahem," said Marco.

"With a little help from Marco, of course," Texas Jake admitted. "One might expect more from a cat who can reeeeeaaaad, but it was good that I was smart enough to take him along, because he was able to distract Steak Knife so that I could get Catnip free. And of course, being the fighter I am, I had to stay behind and fight the whole gang single-pawed, without a bit of help from anyone—"

"Ahem!" said both Marco and Polo together.

"Except for a nosy crow who came diving out of the sky at the very last minute, but even if he hadn't, I assure you, Carlotta my dear, that I would have brought your kitten safely home to you."

"I am grateful to you all," Carlotta purred. "I wonder sometimes what will befall my kittens when they are out on their own, adopted into new homes. How will they hang on to their tails then?"

"My sweet Carlotta, we were young once, remember?" Texas told her. "Our mothers must have said the same thing about us. Our mothers must have worried too."

Polo wondered if that was true—if his own mother had worried about him. Whether she thought about him now.

The cats lay down for the night, still talking about the adventure.

"I never knew rats to work for cats," murmured Elvis. "If they wanted, I'll bet one could eat the other up."

"If they ever put their minds to it, they could join forces and take over the neighborhood," said Boots.

"Minds? What minds?" asked Marco. "Brainless and heartless, that's what they are."

One by one the cats fell asleep as a small shaft of moonlight slowly crossed the floor.

Perhaps because of all the excitement the day before, and because the cats were exhausted, they slept late the next morning. Marco was having the most wonderful dream about a salmon buffet, an "all you can eat" buffet, when suddenly the Sunday silence was interrupted by the sound of a man's voice from down the alley.

"Car-lot-ta! Car-lot-ta!" the voice came.

Carlotta rose up in the rag box and listened, her ears sticking straight up in the air.

"Car-lot-ta!" the voice came, louder now.

"My master!" she meowed in alarm. "It's my master!"

"Will he find you here?" asked Polo.

"I don't know," said the she-cat. "But if he's in the alley, he'll look in every garage. And if he finds us, he will take the kittens to the pound. Or he will take them out in the country and leave them there. He doesn't want them coming home with me, and knows I would never leave them alone."

"There is only one thing to do," said Texas Jake. "Fight."

"Wrong," said Polo, who suddenly had a magnificent idea. "There is something else we could do. We must disguise the kittens."

"How?" cried Carlotta, as her master's voice grew louder still, and they could hear his footsteps on the stones in the alley.

"Every cat take a kitten," Polo directed. "Hide it somehow. It's up to you."

Each of the big cats picked up a kitten by the scruff of its neck.

Marco dropped Hamburger inside a big boot.

Polo hid Scamper beneath an old hat.

Boots put Mustard under a mop.

Elvis dropped Sugar inside a large vase.

And Texas Jake hid Catnip beneath an overturned bucket.

The master's footsteps sounded on the stairs. Carlotta leaped to her feet in panic. Then she jumped to the top of a trunk and from there to the shoulder of an old coat hanging from the rafters, a coat with a fur collar around the neck. She squirmed under the collar until her whole body was stretched out beneath it, and it was hard to tell which was cat and which was collar.

"Be still, now," Texas warned the kittens, and there wasn't a sound from anywhere.

A moment later a tall man appeared in the loft.

"Aha!" he said. "Cats! So this is where they hang out, is it?"

The five male cats who were sprawled lazily on the floor each opened one eye and observed him for a moment, studying the man in the suede jacket, then closed it again.

"Carlotta?" the man said, looking around the loft. "Carlotta?"

Nothing moved. The man began walking about, looking in all the corners, overturning a cardboard box with old magazines in it. Then he stared at the male cats in exasperation. "If you could only talk," he said to Texas, "you could tell me where she is, I'll bet. She's off somewhere with those darn kittens, I'll bet, and I'm not going to have a mess of babies in my house."

He went over and sat down on top of the overturned bucket. Polo swallowed.

"No sireee!" said the man to himself. "Let a cat come home with a litter of kittens, and it won't be long before she's coming home with another. I can put up with the ways and wiles of one cat, but I sure can't put up with two, and I'm not about to turn my house over to six or seven."

Nothing stirred. Hamburger, Scamper, Mustard, Sugar, and Catnip didn't make a peep.

The man focused his eyes on Texas Jake, and as though the big yellow cat could understand—which, of course, he could—said, "Tell her that if she wants her bed back and her china bowl and her fuzzy toys and her porcelain water dish, she had better come home alone."

The fur beneath the fur collar quivered but otherwise did not move.

Carlotta's master reached out with the toe of his shoe and nudged Marco. "What do you fellas do up here all day, huh? Either you're darn good mousers or you go home at night to a square meal, that's for sure. You're a fat one, aren't you?"

Marco hissed and boxed his shoe.

Carlotta's master laughed, and finally stood up. He took one more walk around the loft, unmindful of the fact that the bucket he had been sitting on moved an inch or two across the floor. He peered into boxes and behind old dressers, and once, Polo felt sure he would see Hamburger hiding in the boot. But after a final stretch, the man went back down the stairs, and the cats listened as his footsteps retreated down the alley.

The boot wobbled.

The vase tipped.

The fur collar jiggled.

The hat wiggled.

The bucket skidded.

And the mop began going around in circles.

At last Carlotta called all her kittens out from their hiding places, and they rejoiced that her master had gone.

Polo was puzzled. "Did you ever wonder about the things humans throw away? This master of Carlotta's seems perfectly willing to give away live kittens."

"They throw almost everything away," Boots agreed. "Newspapers, bottles, magazines, paper plates, coupons, little white spoons, razors, tissues, diapers, cameras. . . . They even give their children away when they reach a certain age. That is the biggest mystery of all."

"What?" cried Carlotta. "Who do they give them to?"

"To College," said Boots. "I don't know who College is, but when they get to be eighteen or so, they put their clothes in a suitcase and give them to College."

"How heartless can they be?" exclaimed Carlotta.

"I have even heard, though I can't swear it's true, that if a man gives his daughter to College and she comes back again, he gives her away a second time to a husband," Boots informed them.

"No!" cried all the cats.

"It's the Mystery of Marriage, they tell me," Boots went on. "The daughter dresses in white and her father walks her down a long path, and at the end of the path is her husband. 'Who gives this woman in marriage?' the big boss asks, and the father answers, 'I do.' Then . . . he simply gives her away."

"What is more valuable than a child? What is more valuable than a pet?" cried Polo.

All the cats hunkered down to think, it was just so strange.

"What do you suppose College does with all those children?" asked Elvis.

"Maybe it makes slaves of them, puts them to work," Texas suggested.

"That's it!" said Boots. "I've heard children say so. They come home to visit and say that College works them like slaves."

"Is it better to be a kitten, to be given away to a nice family, or to be a two-legged child and given away to College?" wondered Carlotta.

"A kitten, by far," said Polo.

"True, true," said Elvis.

Marco cleared his throat. "I think," he said, "that college is not a person."

All the cats opened their eyes wide and stared.

"Not a person?" asked Texas Jake. "If College is not a two-legged, what is it?"

"It's . . . um . . . " Marco tried to think what a college was. He had seen pictures of colleges in the newspaper at the bottom of his litter box, but it was hard to say exactly what it was.

"I believe that college is a building," he said at last.

"A building?" sneered Texas Jake. "A *building*? Parents give their children away to a *building*? And the building works them like slaves? Don't make me laugh. For a cat who can reeeeaaaad, you don't know very much. No sir, not very much at all."

The cats began to smile and then to chuckle and then to laugh out loud at the silliness of the suggestion. Laughing helped them forget that they had yet to find five good homes for the five little kittens, or Carlotta's master would send them away, and it wouldn't be to college.

Nineteen
The Kittens' Song

It was time for breakfast at the Fishmonger. The cats had not eaten for many hours, and Carlotta was feeling a little weak. It wasn't spring yet, but the sun was out, the sunniest day in weeks.

When all the cats and kittens had gathered at the restaurant, the Abyssinian got up on the wall and announced that the cat quartet had been working on a good-bye song for Carlotta's kittens.

"But they aren't gone yet!" Carlotta protested, nibbling her salmon fillet.

"They will be shortly, one way or another," the Abyssinian purred. "We all know what happens to kittens. If good homes aren't found within a reasonable time, they just . . . disappear."

"And so," said the Siamese, crawling up on the wall beside him, "we have composed a little song."

At that, Elvis too joined the singers, along with the

Persian, and after tuning up with a yowl or two, the cats began:

"Oh, kittens five,
To keep alive
We all must say good-bye.
For if you stay
Another day
There's every chance you'll die."

"Now, just a minute . . . !" Texas Jake protested, as Carlotta began to weep. But the cat quartet sang on:

"They'll put you
In a paper bag
And weigh you down with stones,
And drown you
In a river till
There's nothing left but bones."

"What is the meaning of this?" thundered Texas. "Is this a proper song to sing to a young mother?" But even he couldn't stop the song:

"But if we find
A house so fine
That's friendly to a cat,
You all may stay
Another day
And grow unusually fat.

"So let us wish
A supper dish
For every kitten here,
And chicken bones
In friendly homes
With warmth and love and cheer.

"And if and when
You come again,
To visit with each other,
Stay awhile
To bring a smile
To her, your little mother."

Carlotta seemed to find peace in the suggestion that her kittens might come back to visit her, so began eating again, and when she was done, she lazily licked her paws.

As the cats made their way back to the loft later, however, they realized that they could not put it off any longer—the unpleasant task of finding homes for Carlotta's kittens.

Texas Jake faced the others. "Go!" he said to Boots and Elvis and Marco and Polo. "And don't come back until you've each found a home. I myself will look for one also. If we can each come up with a family that will take a cat, then all five kittens will be provided for."

So the cats set out, not very confidently at all, each going a different way.

Texas crossed the street by the Fishmonger and surveyed the town houses that sat in a row on the other side.

Elvis went up on every porch of every house for the next two blocks, peering in each window, while Boots did the same in the other direction. Marco checked the backyards of all the houses on either side of the big house where the Neals lived.

Polo, however, had no idea in the world where he should look. He was so used to doing everything with Marco that he wasn't at all sure he could think for himself. If Marco told him to jump, he jumped. If Marco told him to eat, he ate. At every house he started to investigate, he saw that one of the other cats had got there first, so he continued walking—up the streets and down the alleys—until he was quite muddled, and didn't know exactly where he was.

He came to a yard where a young boy was hitting a rubber tire with a baseball bat—*whack, whack.* That didn't seem to be a place for a kitten.

He came to a yard where the children were quarreling.

"You said I could have the swing next!" cried one girl.

"I did not! You had it longest yesterday, so I get it today!" yelled her brother.

"I haven't had a turn at all!" screeched another.

"Oh, shut up, Sally! You always get the best of everything!" said the first girl.

Polo went on. No place for a kitten there.

In another yard there were already two dogs; in another, five children were fighting and crying. Some homes had messy yards with junk piled everywhere. Some were so neat and trim that a kitten would never be allowed to dig even a tiny hole.

At the next corner, Polo jumped up on the low wall that

surrounded a large yellow house, thinking no one was in the yard because everything was so quiet. He was quite surprised to find that there was not only one person sitting in the yard, but four.

There were two elderly women on a bench with their hands in their laps.

There was a large man in a wheelchair, with his arms at his sides.

And a tiny little woman in a brown coat was walking back and forth and seemed to be talking to herself, for no one paid a bit of attention.

What sort of place is this? Polo wondered, where everyone seemed so quiet and sad, except for the little old lady who talked to herself.

At that moment the back door of the big house opened and a woman dressed in a pink smock and pants came out and put a sweater around one of the women on the bench.

"How are you doing, Mr. Grimwald?" she said to the man in the wheelchair. "Isn't it a nice day to be out in the sun? There will be leaves on the trees before you know it." And then, to the second woman on the bench, she said, "I wonder if those cardinals will come back this year and build a nest in the thicket."

But the two women on the bench did not answer, and the man in the wheelchair didn't even blink his eyes. The little woman in the brown coat went right on walking and talking to herself.

The woman in the pink smock looked about her and sighed, shaking her head before she went back inside.

And it was right at that moment that Polo knew. He

knew that what this home needed was something to make people smile. Something to make them laugh. This was the place for Carlotta's kittens.

He jumped down off the wall and began to run up the block. At the next corner he turned left. Then he turned right. Then he turned completely around and even walked backward ten steps before he realized that he was lost and had no idea in the world how to get back to Murphy's garage.

I'm hopeless, Polo told himself. *I can't do anything without Marco.* He went this way and that. Backward and forward. It wasn't until he heard a sound—a low sound, a fearful sound—that Polo knew he was close to home. He jumped up on a fence to get a better look and found himself looking right down into the jowls of Bertram the Bad.

The big mastiff began to bark furiously as it raced along the fence. Polo raced along the top even faster, however. He leaped to the fence of the neighboring lot, around a tree, over a shed, and finally, finally, he saw the Fishmonger off in the distance, and from there he found his way back to Murphy's garage.

The other cats were just arriving when he got there, and Polo, out of breath, had to wait a few minutes before he could speak.

"Well?" said Texas Jake to the others.

"I didn't find a thing," said Boots. "I *looked,* Texas! I investigated every home within three blocks, and couldn't find one that seemed a good place for one of Carlotta's kittens."

"Me either," said Marco. "There was one home with a small child in it that I thought would do, but there was already a kitten, and the kid was holding it up by its neck."

All the cats groaned.

"I *thought* I'd found a place, until I saw two huge dogs there at the back door," said Elvis. "They could swallow a kitten in one gulp."

"I didn't have any luck either," Texas Jake confessed. He looked at Polo. "And you?"

"I found a home, I think!" said Polo. "A place that needs a smile. A place that needs a kitten. *Five* kittens, even!"

Carlotta sat up and looked at Polo admiringly. All the cats looked at him.

"Where?" asked Marco. "Where is this house?"

Polo huddled down on top of the newspapers and looked timidly about him. "I don't know," he said. "I forgot where it is."

Twenty
Good-bye, Good-bye . . .

Polo, how can you be so stupid?" Marco asked him. "You found a place that would take all the kittens, but you can't remember where it is? Didn't you get the address?"

"I can't read," said Polo.

"Oh. Right," said Marco.

"A cat doesn't need to read to remember," Texas boomed. "You have eyes, don't you, Polo? You have ears! You have a nose! What did the place look like?"

"Like a place that needed a smile," Polo answered.

"What did it sound like?"

"It didn't sound like anything at all, except for one little old lady chirping like a sparrow. It sounded like a place that could use a mew."

"Well, what did it *smell* like?" asked Texas.

"Like . . . like old men's shaving cream and lilac perfume," said Polo.

"Great! Just great!" said Elvis. "We have to go out looking for a place that sounds like a sparrow, smells like shaving cream, and looks like it could use a smile."

"Well, at least he did better than any of us did," said Marco, standing up for his brother. "Let's wake the kittens and go looking."

Carlotta gently moved her body and roused her sleeping kittens, who were sprawled this way and that across her belly.

"Wake up, my darlings," she said. "There's a big wide world out there, and it's waiting just for you."

One by one the kittens yawned and got up on their sturdy little legs.

"Where are we going?" asked Hamburger.

"To a place you have never been before," his mother answered.

"What does it look like?" asked Scamper.

"Like a place that needs a kitten," said Carlotta.

"What will we do there?" Mustard wanted to know.

"Everything that you do here, only better," Carlotta said. "Because it will be your new home."

"Are you coming too?" asked Sugar.

"For a little while," said Carlotta.

"And then you're going to leave us?" asked Catnip, beginning to wail.

"I will hold you forever in my heart, and I will visit now and then," said Carlotta. "Come now. Follow the others."

Down the stairs of the loft the procession went, out the garage door, then down the alley toward the Fishmonger.

"Now, *think!*" Texas Jake said to Polo. "This morning, when we all separated to look for a home for the kittens, which way did you go?"

Polo tried to think. "I went in every direction there is," he said. "I made turns. I went left and I went right. I even walked backward for a while."

"But which direction did you go in first?" Elvis insisted.

Polo thought. Finally he began walking, and the cats and kittens followed. This way, that way, backward and forward. But suddenly he stopped and said, "Listen!"

Everyone listened. At first they heard nothing. Then there came a soft, high sound, like a sparrow chirping. With pounding heart, Polo led the way as the sound grew a little louder, the houses looked a bit more familiar, and finally, straight ahead, was the low wall surrounding the big house.

There in the yard as before was the man in the wheelchair, the two women on the bench, and the sparrow lady talking to herself. But this time there were even more people in the yard, elderly people sitting in folding chairs, enjoying the early spring sunshine. None of them was talking, however, except the sparrow woman. No one was smiling.

"This is it," said Polo, as the cats jumped up on the low wall surrounding the house.

The kittens looked at their mother, and she licked each one on the head. "Always look out for each other," she said.

"Look both ways before crossing a street," said Boots.

"Never get your tails caught in a screen door," said Marco.

"Don't forget to wash behind your ears," said Elvis.

"A mouse goes down better headfirst," said Texas Jake.

"Any mouse but Timothy," added Polo.

One by one the kittens jumped up on the wall. One by one they jumped down into the garden. They headed for the circle where the old people were sitting.

Hamburger began chasing a cricket.

Scamper began chasing his tail.

Mustard and Sugar rolled about in the grass, wrestling and nipping at each other's ears, while Catnip simply strolled over to the man in the wheelchair and brushed against his leg, purring loudly.

The sparrow woman stopped chirping and stared. "Look! Look!" she cried, pointing.

The two women on the bench began to smile.

The man in the wheelchair laughed out loud and reached down to pat Catnip on the head.

The other men and women who were sitting on folding chairs began to laugh and point, and soon they were bending down, inviting the kittens to come over and be petted.

The back door opened and the woman in pink came out.

"Well, would you look at that!" she said, and then called, "Edna! Grace! Come out here and see what we've got!"

Another woman in pink came out. Then another.

Finally a man in a white coat came to the door. He saw the kittens playing. He heard the men and women laughing. "Just what the doctor ordered," he said.

"Let's put out some food," said one of the women in pink.

"Let's make them a little bed," said another.

Carlotta turned away.

"I want to go home," she said. "I want to remember them always just as I saw them now."

"Your kittens aren't that far away," said Polo. "They'll come to the Fishmonger every now and then."

"I'm sure of it," Carlotta said.

It was time, the cats knew, for Carlotta to go home

without her kittens. Time for the he-cats, too, to make their way back to their masters to be fed and groomed. The first time Marco and Polo had made their grand escape from the Neals' comfortable house where they had been raised since they were kittens, the Neals had thought they were gone for good, and had taken in two new little kittens, Jumper and Spinner. So now the tabbies had to share their house, their water dish, and their velveteen basket with the new arrivals, and they didn't want to stay away so long they might discover that two *more* pets had been added to the family.

"Good-bye, Carlotta!" the he-cats all said to the dainty calico cat as she rubbed noses with each of them. "When spring is here and the moon is full, we'll meet again in Murphy's garage and have a new adventure."

"Every day is a new adventure for me," said Carlotta, and with a perky flip of her tail, she walked down the alley toward home, one paw in front of the next.

"What mystery shall we work on when we come back again?" asked Marco, fondly watching her go.

"Where do kittens come from?" suggested Polo. "How about that? We know they came from Carlotta, but why don't *we* have kittens?"

"Perhaps it's something she ate," said Elvis, as Carlotta's tail disappeared around the corner.

"Perhaps it's something she drank," said Boots.

"Wrong! Wrong! Wrong!" said Texas Jake. "Don't you cats know anything at all? Carlotta has kittens and we don't because she is female. All females are born with tiny seeds inside them, and every so often, when the seasons change perhaps, the seeds become kittens, and out they come."

"Oh," said Marco, for even he, the cat who could read, didn't know the answer to that.

"Good-bye," all the cats said to each other. "We'll meet again when the moon is full."

The two tabby brothers went down the alley in the other direction. It was too early for dinner at the Neals', but not too early for a nap. They walked to the white picket fence, nudged open the gate, then went up the steps to the back door. Marco meowed, and Polo joined in.

After a while the door opened, and Mrs. Neal looked them over.

"Well, you finally decided to come home, did you?" she said, as Marco and Polo strolled inside, tails high in the air. "I certainly would like to know where you've been all this time, and what you *do* when you're gone."

They would gladly have told her, of course, but to her, their talk was only meowing, so they went out to the sun porch to take a nap. The younger cats, Jumper and Spinner, however, were themselves asleep in the velveteen basket, and merely opened one eye apiece as Marco walked over and gave the basket a nudge.

"Consider yourselves lucky," said Marco to the kittens.

Spinner opened both eyes. "Why?" he asked.

"That you were adopted, when you *could* have been tied up in a sack . . ."

"What?" cried Jumper.

"Weighted down with stones . . . ," added Polo.

"And dumped in the river," Marco finished.

The kittens looked about them in alarm.

"Somewhere," Marco continued, "your mother is wondering whatever happened to the little kittens she once